Hadi's Journey

S0-AAZ-482

Jennifer Bond Reed

iUniverse, Inc.
New York Lincoln Shanghai

Hadi's Journey

All Rights Reserved © 2003 by Jennifer Bond Reed

No part of this book may be reproduced or transmitted in any form or by any means, graphic, electronic, or mechanical, including photocopying, recording, taping, or by any information storage retrieval system, without the written permission of the publisher.

iUniverse, Inc.

For information address:
iUniverse, Inc.
2021 Pine Lake Road, Suite 100
Lincoln, NE 68512
www.iuniverse.com

This is a work of fiction. The characters, incidents, and dialogues in this book are products of the author's imagination and are not to be construed as real. Any resemblance to actual events or persons, living or dead, is entirely coincidental.

ISBN: 0-595-29375-1

Printed in the United States of America

Dedicated to the boys and girls who have been exploited by camel racing.

Contents

Chapter 1:   Kidnapped 1

Chapter 2:   The Camel Souk 11

Chapter 3:   The First Day 19

Chapter 4:   A New Friend 25

Chapter 5:   Master Aziz and the Stranger 32

Chapter 6:   Training 43

Chapter 7:   Hadi's Turn 51

Chapter 8:   Recovery 59

Chapter 9:   The Great Camel Race 63

Chapter 10: Hadi's Plan 72

Chapter 11: The Escape 77

Chapter 12: Homeward Bound 82

Chapter 13: Home At Last! 86

Author's Notes 97

Hadi's Journey

Chapter 1

Kidnapped

═══════════════════════════════════════

"Don't forget, Hadi. You have to clean the chicken pen after you've gathered the eggs. Then you need to watch the children while I go to market."

Hadi watched his mother as she scrambled about the one room, mud walled shack they called home. His little sister, Samra, cried in the corner. Her blue dress was dirty and torn and she looked up at Hadi with big brown eyes, soaked in tears. Hadi picked her up. "But, Mama. I have too much to do," he said rubbing his little sister's back. She was heavy in her arms but she had stopped crying.

"Don't argue with me!" his mother shouted. She stood up straight and wiped her brow. "I have enough to do this morning, Hadi. You're the oldest and you need to help."

Standing in the doorway, Hadi's younger brother snickered.

"Shut up, Hasan." Hadi rushed to him and pushed him out of the door. Still holding his sister, he quickly put her to the ground and marched off. As he went to the chicken's pen, he heard Samra wail and his brother laugh. He walked across a dirt yard to a makeshift pen. Inside the wire and boards were four chickens. Hadi grabbed a small shovel, climbed inside and scooped out the manure. He threw it into a pile that would be used for fertilizing their small garden. Then he threw chicken feed on the ground.

As the chickens raced to eat, Hadi tripped over one trying to get out. He landed on the ground and skinned his knee. Slowly blood oozed from the scrape. "Darn it!" he said and wiped the blood with his dirty hand.

"Hadi!" his mother yelled from the other side of the yard. "I need to go. Hurry up!" Again, Hadi heard his sister cry. He covered his ears wishing he could block it all out.

"If only I didn't live here," he mumbled under his breath. He looked again at his knee. It stung now and dark red blood drizzled down his shin. He left it and escaped the coop.

"Mama, why don't I go for you," he suggested as he walked up to her.

"What happened to your leg?" she asked, not answering his question.

"It's just a scrape. Can I go to the market? I don't want to stay home again with them." Hadi pointed to the small group of children. His sister Samra was the youngest. She was just three years old. Hasan was next. He was five. Omar was seven and Hadi, the oldest, was nine.

His mother looked at him and squinted her eyes as if she were thinking. "Please, Mama. I want to go. I need a break from everything."

"I don't know, Hadi. You aren't really old enough. It's dangerous out there. I don't think so." She bent over to pick up a bag.

Hadi stomped his foot down. "I want to go!" he demanded with his hands on his hips. His mother twirled around so quickly Hadi thought she was going to grab him. "I mean, I'm old enough. I can do this. *Please.*" He folded his hands together and begged. "Besides, it will help you out too, won't it?"

Hadi's mother handed him the bag with one hand and two coins with the other. "Just this once and only because my feet hurt and the walk is too long."

Hadi grabbed the bag. "Besides, you are annoying me today." She smiled at Hadi. "Hurry back!" shouted his mother as Hadi raced down the dirt road that led to the village.

Without looking back Hadi waved his arm in the air. In his hand, he grasped two small coins; just enough to buy some curry the family needed at the market. He felt each foot hit the ground with a soft thud as he ran down the narrow dirt road. He passed a narrow canal carrying water to a nearby field. Just ahead was a neighbor's small farm. "I can't slow down," he said under his breath. He was glad to be out of the house; away from the chores and his brothers and sisters! His heart raced and beat in time with each step he took. He passed the neighbor's house also made of stone and mud with a thatched roof, before turning a corner and slowed to a walk. A sharp cramp in his side forced him to stop. It was another mile to the market and there was no way Hadi could keep up the pace. For a nine year old, he was small. Although he was in good shape and fit, the humid air hung around him like a heavy blanket, weighing him down.

Hadi stopped and looked up into the sun. He kicked a small rock with his foot. "Finally, I'm out of there!" he shouted so the world could hear. Sweat glistened on his brown skin and dripped off the bottom of his cheek. He coughed and spit onto the ground and rolled his head around in circles. "If I keep walking, this cramp should go away." He took a few steps forward. With his dirty right hand, he squeezed the side of his body trying to rub the cramp out. He kept on walking.

Feeling resentful, Hadi kicked the dirt some more and watched chunks of it fall heavily to the ground. "I hate being the oldest!" His brothers and sisters got to stay home where they could play and only had a few chores to do each day. Not Hadi. Being the oldest child of four, he was the one who had the most responsibility, aside from his parents. Hadi had to get up early, feed the livestock, clean their pens, get the younger children ready for the day and often, he had to watch them while his father and mother went to work. Today, he wanted to go to the market, by himself. Mostly he wanted to be away from his family and the work. Hadi enjoyed being on his own and having some peace and quiet. His mother wasn't feeling well either and she was more irritable than usual. She hurt her foot in the fields when she stepped on a jagged rock. It caused an infection and she couldn't walk for days. Father worked in the fields too.

Hadi kicked the dirt with his bare foot one more time and uncovered an unusual looking brown rock. He reached down and picked it up. Turning it around in his hands, it had shiny flecks that reflected the sun's light and sparkled. "This one's worth saving," he said and stuffed the rock into a pocket in his salwar. A goat swaggered in front of him, and cried in disgust as if Hadi were in his way.

"Baa, baa!"

"Shoo! Get home," Hadi said to the goat and chased it off the road.

Staying close to the side of the road, Hadi was prepared to jump to the side and huddle down as low as he could if he saw a stranger. His parents had spent many evenings talking to Hadi and his brothers about the strange men who visited villages. They came from other countries and took children right off the streets. With lots of lecturing, Hadi's mother warned him of the danger and told him what to do. A chill ran up Hadi's spine. Many children had been kidnapped in the village recently and Hadi didn't want to be one of them. He knew he was old enough to take care of himself. "Besides," he thought, "I'm too quick!" He remembered what his mother told him before they went together on trips to the market.

"When we go to the village you stay close to me."

"What if someone grabs me?" Hadi asked.

"You scream as loud as you can," said his mother.

Hadi jingled the coins in his hand and wiped his forehead. The cramp soon worked its way out and Hadi saw the thatched rooftops and white and brown walls of the village's homes and shops ahead.

Farther beyond grey jagged mountain tops jetted skyward. Hadi often sat and stared at them. One day he would climb to the top and maybe touch heaven!

Not only was it hot but it was monsoon season. The Chenab River, which flowed nearby had recently flooded and some areas were still muddy. It had rained nearly every day. Cypress trees lined the road, their green leaves dripped with water. The stench of cow manure fermenting in the sun lingered in the air. Hadi crinkled his nose at the smell. Today it seemed particularly strong. Ruffled voices of people buying and selling their goods beckoned him closer. He gripped the coins tightly, raised his head and focused his dark brown eyes towards the village. "Get the curry and head right back home," he told himself. Hadi, with ripped brown pants and a soiled white shirt marched barefoot into town. He felt like a soldier on a mission.

He knew where they sold the curry and it wasn't much further. Suddenly, like a flood, Hadi was drawn into crowds of people. He was pushed to the right and then to the left. Men jeered at him as he made his way through. Hadi refused to make eye contact with anyone. He felt the mud ooze between his toes and knew it was not just mud made of water and dirt. Most likely, he was stepping in cow manure and other droppings left behind by all sorts of animals, cows, dogs, cats and chickens that roamed the streets.

Vendors sat in garage-like stalls with their goods lying on tables and over-turned baskets. Hadi squinted as one man cut the throat of a chicken and tipped it upside down in the street to drain the blood. A hot fire nearby sizzled with pieces of chicken. Hadi's stomach grumbled and as much as he would have liked to use the money his mother gave him to buy a piece of meat, he remembered his objective-get the curry and get out! A horn honked loudly many times and shouts from men echoed throughout the busy village. Pushed from one side to another he spotted a man selling brightly colored fabric. A newly made kameez made of soft sapphire blue fabric, swayed in the breeze. It reminded Hadi of a kite.

"I'm almost there," he said as he raced up to the man selling the curry. Standing against the side of a falling down shack, the man seemed tall to Hadi. He had a moustache and thick black hair parted to one side. He smiled at Hadi.

"I'd like to buy some curry." Hadi held out his hand and showed the man the two coins. The man grabbed the coins and shoved them into his pocket. He filled a small sack with the rich smelling spice. Hadi watched as some spilled over the sides of the sack and fell to the ground without a sound. The man poured the curry as if it were water and when he was finished, he tied the sack with string and handed it to Hadi.

"Be careful, boy. Get home quickly. This isn't a place for a child. See that car?" He pointed through a clearing of people. A gray car was parked on the side of the road. Hadi nodded.

"There are bad people in that car." The man leaned back against the building, which creaked with his weight.

Slowly Hadi turned and faced the crowd of people. He walked away from the car. A group of children played in the dirt drawing circles with the handle of an old broom. Men huddled together and talked about the latest news. Hadi only saw a couple of women carrying bags and lingering from one vendor to another. Mostly, it was all men. Taller than he, they blocked Hadi's view of the road in front of him. He stood on tip toe to get a better look but too easily lost his balance. People pushed him again and he nearly lost his curry. He held onto it tightly. His heart pounded and suddenly he was scared. He just wanted to be home, where he was safe. "I'm never coming back here again by myself," he mumbled, hurrying to the clearing in the road. He stepped in the chicken's blood and kept his focus only on getting home. A tear streaked down his face leaving a grimy trail. He quickly wiped it away and walked faster through the crowd.

Just a few steps away the road cleared. Another mile and Hadi would be safe at home with his mother, brothers and sister. His heart raced at the thought and the urgency to get there spurred him forward. As he took one step then another his body was suddenly twisted back. He felt a hand cover his mouth and another firmly grabbed his shoulders. Hadi tried to scream just as his mother told him. What came out was muffled in a hand. With the crowd of people behind him, he kicked and writhed and twisted his body like a snake. Another set of hands held him down. Hadi looked at the two men who grabbed him. Fear paralyzed his legs and he could hardly move. It didn't matter. Hadi was small and the men were big and strong. He dropped the sack of curry.

The gray car Hadi had seen earlier slowly moved forward. One of the men reached over to open the door. As he did, the other man shoved Hadi inside. "Let me go!" he screamed. A sharp slap pierced his face and stung his skin. The men climbed in beside him and sat down. They covered his mouth with tape and pushed him down in the seat.

"Got the papers?" asked one of the men to the driver.

"Hold on, let me get out of here," the driver shouted.

Hadi heard the car horn honk to get people and cows out of the way. It sped up and rumbled down the bumpy road. Hadi buckled over in pain. His face stung and his body trembled. He thought of his mother waiting for him back home. *What am I going to do?* he wondered and quietly sobbed. The tape was pulling the skin on either side of his face and breathing was hard. Hadi pushed air in and out of his nose and he felt like he could suffocate.

Once the car was out of town, the driver handed a set of papers to the men next to Hadi.

"Ah, good," said the man on Hadi's right side. "This is a fine birth certificate. Now you are my son." The man ruffled Hadi's hair and chuckled. Then he ripped the tape off Hadi's mouth and flung it out the window. He reached into his pocket and pulled out some money. The driver quickly reached back and grabbed it.

Hadi's lips stung. He ran his tongue over them and tasted salty blood. He rubbed his mouth briskly. The only other time he had felt so much pain was when they were building the fence for the chicken coop. His brother accidentally whacked Hadi in the face with a pole and knocked him out. His lips swelled so they looked like a cow's lips.

Hadi stayed hunched down and quiet as he listened to the men talk. The problem was, he didn't understand a word they were saying. Hours went by. Hadi stared out the window and watched kids playing on the side of the road in towns he had never seen. The rickety old car sped by small villages, an occasional herd of cows or sheep. Finally, he asked in a whisper, "Where are you taking me?" He barely got the words beyond his sore lips.

The man to his right looked at Hadi. "Some place better than this rat hole," he said and laughed. The car hit a pothole and bounced Hadi and the men up and down. "Take it easy," said the man pushing on the back of the front seat.

"It's not a rat hole!" Hadi shouted. "It's my home!"

"Shut your mouth," said the man and he squeezed Hadi's mouth tightly.

Looking out the window Hadi saw a river. They followed it for miles. Signs marked where they were but Hadi couldn't read. "Where are we now?" he asked.

"Near Karachi," said the driver. "You won't be staying there either."

Hadi's mouth was dry and he had to go to the bathroom. "Can we stop to get a drink?" *Maybe I can run away then*, he thought. "I need to go to the bathroom."

No one said a word. Everyone looked straight out the front window of the car.

Hadi closed his eyes again and laid his head on the back of the seat. *This isn't happening.* His mother warned him, so did the man selling curry. Anger flooded his body. *If I hadn't begged Mama to let me go to the market, I wouldn't be here*, he thought. Picturing his mother brought tears to his eyes. He wanted to be home with his family. Hadi kept his eyes shut.

Late that night the car came to Karachi. The smell of salt air tickled Hadi's nose. He awoke, rubbing his eyes trying to make things out. Bright lights blinded him but he could see movement ahead of him.

"We're in Karachi," said the driver with a scowl. "Get out. You must hurry before the boat leaves."

The two men pushed Hadi out the door. He nearly fell but one man caught him by the shoulders. "Ouch, that hurts!" Hadi cried.

The driver glared at Hadi, put the car in reverse and sped off. Sandwiched between the two men, Hadi was hustled down a wooden ramp. He heard the gentle lapping of waves as they hit the docks. "Are we in Karachi?" he asked and wriggled trying to break free. "I want to go home!" he yelled yet just as soon as those words had left his mouth, a hand covered it. Hadi's eyes darted around. He noticed many other young boys all hurrying in the same direction. Some cried out but their words went unheard or unnoticed, Hadi didn't know which. Little boys younger than him were perched on the backs of some men. They clung tightly to the men's shoulders afraid of falling off. Hadi looked at them. Their eyes were filled with fear as they stared back.

A small wooden boat was docked at the end of the pier with its motor running. Hadi noticed smoke rising from its motor and the smell of gas fumes permeated the salty air. *It's not big enough to fit all these people. Maybe the dark is hiding the other half of the boat,* he thought. He walked up the ramp with everyone else. Boys pushed and cried and the strange men in the night shouted at them to be quiet.

Pushed aboard, Hadi was shoved to the far corner of the boat. He looked over the edge into the dark water. Lights from the boat and on the dock reflected off the water. The two men stood by him, glaring at him often. Hadi didn't dare to move or speak. He looked ahead as the boys clamored aboard, one by one, some stolen that day from their families or the only homes they knew, the streets of their poor villages. Other children were accompanied by their father or an uncle. The sad look on their faces told Hadi, none wanted to be there.

"Why me?" Hadi whispered. As he was pushed down to the floor of the boat all his physical problems of wanting to eat and drink and go to the bathroom were gone. All he wanted was to be at home with his family. The motor revved and stirred the water so it splashed cold drops onto Hadi and the other passengers. Shouts from the cabin echoed in the night but Hadi didn't understand what they were saying. They spoke in a different language from his own. He looked towards the cabin. A man lit a cigarette and with the light from the match, Hadi made out the face of someone who looked more cold than the two who had kidnapped him. A white turban covered his head and a deep dark beard came to a point at the bottom of his chin. His eyes surveyed the cargo and squinted as if he were counting and thinking about the boys on his boat. He shouted some words, the lines were brought in and the small boat sputtered quietly into the darkness of the night.

Only the soft purr of the motor and quiet whimpers of boys were heard. Too afraid to rebel or speak or cry, Hadi covered his head with his hands and tried to shut down the emotions of his heart so he couldn't feel anymore pain. It didn't work. He pictured his mother and father pacing the small dirt floor of their home worried that Hadi had not returned. He knew his mother would cry herself to sleep that night and suddenly Hadi realized just how much he loved his family despite all the work he had to do, and despite his responsibilities.

"No matter what," Hadi whispered, "I will get home."

Chapter 2

The Camel Souk

An hour into the boat ride, the whimpers of young boys subsided. Hadi looked up. Many boys had fallen asleep, their bodies leaning against each other. They looked like sacks of rice all piled in lumps across the floor of the boat. Only the faint light from the cabin allowed Hadi to make out their shapes. Two men inside the cabin puffed on cigarettes and laughed and talked in between inhales.

Hadi looked at the man on his right side. The man looked back without a smile. "Can you at least tell me where I'm going?" Hadi asked.

The man sat up a little straighter and looked ahead. "You're going to Abu Dhabi," he said. "To work in a camel souk."

"What's that?" Hadi looked at the man.

"It's a market place where they take care of camels. No more questions, little rat. If you aren't quiet, I'll throw you overboard and let the sharks deal with you."

Hadi backed away and peered over the side of the boat. The water was dark as coffee and cold. He didn't want to be shark bait so he stopped asking questions. He couldn't believe he was going to a strange country to work! He grabbed his stomach as it flip flopped from the up and down motion of the boat. Hadi had never been at sea, let alone on a boat so small with that many people. He grabbed his stomach and waited for the next wave to come.

Quickly he leaned over the rail leaned over the rail. He threw up until no more would come. His head burned and sweat mixed with his tears. *If I jump overboard, maybe I can swim back,* he thought looking out over the black water. There was no way. He couldn't see any lights from the shore now. Darkness hung like a black curtain over everything. Just then, one of the men pulled him down from the rail.

Hadi sat for hours staring into the night. He wondered about where he was going; what it would be like. He thought about home too. His family, he imagined, was sound asleep except that there was a small space, empty and cold where Hadi should be.

Suddenly, the man who was accompanying him pulled on his sleeve. "We're here," he said, pointing to the other side of the boat. It was still dark but Hadi could see lights twinkling like stars as the harbor of Abu Dhabi came closer. On the horizon, the first slivers of sun rise looked like gold. It was a new day but to Hadi it offered no comfort or hope. His legs wobbled as he tried to stand up. The boat slowed and its engines roared loudly one last time sending a wave of smoke up and over the passengers. Hadi coughed. The fumes were making him sick. He grabbed a hold of the side of the boat just as it hit the dock. Men shouted directions and lines were thrown over. The gas filled fumes combined with the rocking and jolting of the boat were too much for Hadi. His legs gave out and he collapsed on the floor. He saw and felt nothing until he awoke inside a cool, air-conditioned bus.

Hadi sat up in his seat. The sun on the rise blinded him at first. "Where am I?" he asked rubbing his eyes. Only one man sat with him in the seat and Hadi didn't know what happened to the other man who had kidnapped him in the village. He caught a glimpse of a palm tree and behind that one an entire row. Palms lined the main city street. To Hadi, it was beautiful. Green palm trees, green grass and gardens looked liked an oasis against the white buildings. White mosques shined like gems under the bright sun.

"Are we at the souk?" Hadi rubbed the sleep out of his eyes and looked at the man next to him.

He grinned, but it wasn't a warm, good morning kind of grin. "You stupid kid. You passed out. Been out for an hour. I had to carry you off the boat. Don't you think I'm as tired and thirsty as you?" He slumped down in the seat and leaned in close to Hadi. "You better not do that at the souk. You're worth a lot of money, boy."

Hadi turned away and looked back out the window. His chin quivered. *I'm not going to cry*, he told himself. His stomach ached from hunger and the time he had heaved. His mouth felt like sandpaper and the lack of food or water made him feel lightheaded. The bus drove right through the lush green city to the outskirts and headed straight for the desert.

Hadi's heart sank when he saw the sand stretched out for miles. Heat waves danced in the distance. There were tall fences on either side of the road. Wisps of brown scrub dotted the land and sand drifted all around. Hadi didn't see grass or bushes or trees of green. He looked behind him as the city of Abu Dhabi faded in with the dancing heat waves. It was as if they were waving goodbye.

"What are the fences for?" asked Hadi. He didn't look at the man when he asked. No, it was best not to look at him.

"To keep the wild camels from getting close to the road."

Wild camels! Hadi searched the barren desert for a wild camel and suddenly there in the distance, wiggling in the waves of heat that rose from the ground, he saw a small herd. Big brown beasts grazing in the scrub slowly walked towards the road. The bus zoomed by but Hadi kept looking for more herds. He didn't see any more as the bus rolled smoothly down the road for many miles.

Half an hour later, the bus slowed and pulled down a bumpy dirty road, leaving a plume of dust behind it. Hadi stretched his neck to see over the heads and out the windows. Small brown houses were lined up side by side. Young boys walked in and out of them through doorways covered by a blanket.

One building stood majestically overlooking all the others. It looked like a great mosque to Hadi. It was a square building with a flat roof. Running along all four sides of the roof were triangular points like a small fence around the rooftop. Windows shaped like squares and triangles were placed here and there on the sides of the building. Hadi scrunched his nose against the windowpane. *It's a funny looking place,* he thought. *I wonder who lives there?*

Palm, olive and date trees dotted the area, offering little shade. Camels in crude corrals munched on mounds of hay and lazily looked up to see the bus pass by. Hadi noticed many corrals filled with camels. Some were lying down while others stood. Occasionally they shook their bodies or swatted a tail to shoo away flies. They all looked bored to Hadi.

Many young boys like himself scurried around like ants, carrying buckets of water, hay and shovels. The fences holding the camels were made from barbed wire and string. Most were ready to fall down.

"Is this where we are going to work?" asked Hadi, hoping the man would say no.

"Lovely, isn't it?" the man said and laughed. "Welcome to the camel souk, boy. Your new home!"

Hadi took one last quick look out the window. He was scared and wanted to crouch in the seat and not get off the bus. This was impossible, thanks to the man who had already grabbed his arm. Finally, the bus squeaked to a stop. The journey had ended. The young boys and their captors filed off the bus and stood in a line. Hadi's legs shook so violently he fell to the ground.

"Get up!" The man slapped his face a few times and shook his shoulders.

Hadi could barely open his eyes.

"Water," said Hadi gasping to get the words out. "Please, I need water."

Hadi watched as the man called for help. "Does anyone have some water for this boy?"

A man a few places up in the line turned and held up a bottle. He hurried over and lifted Hadi's head. He poured the water into Hadi's mouth and drizzled it on his head. "He is not used to this hot air," said Hadi's captor.

"It is different from the Bangladesh heat," said the man with the water bottle. "That is where I am from. At least there is plenty of water back home. Here these boys will drink sand."

Hadi opened his mouth wide not wanting to waste a drop. The cold liquid flowed down his throat.

"Can you get up?" The man held out a hand.

"Yes, I think so." Hadi slowly got up. His legs shook but the water had helped. He followed the slow moving line inside the building that looked like a mosque.

"If you do that again or ask for anything else, you'll be sorry. Stand tall and look strong, boy or else..." The man grabbed his arm and squeezed it tightly.

As they walked inside, Hadi noticed immediately the change in temperature. With the sun off his head, the air inside was much cooler. Inside a grand hall, Hadi looked at the rugs hanging on the wall. They were made in beautiful hues of blue and gold, with white silk flowers. To the right was a room where the boys were entering. The walls were brown like the outside of the building and heavy wooden doors on either side of the large room remained closed. Hadi wondered what treasures lay behind the closed doors.

All the men and boys filed one by one to a long desk that was covered with piles of white and tan colored clothing. The first person they met was a man with a turban on his head and a black beard as thick as tar. He held a clipboard and pen. He looked just like the man on the boat.

"Name?" asked the man.

Hadi felt weak again as he looked up at the man.

"Ha, Ha, Hadi," he stuttered.

His captor shoved papers in front of the man. "He's my son. I am letting him stay here, while I work in town."

Hadi felt his insides burn. He was not his son and wanted to say so. His captor put his arm around Hadi and pulled him close. He smiled at Hadi.

"You from Multan?" asked the man. He never looked up from his sheets of papers and Hadi watched as he scribbled something down.

"Yes, sir."

The man ripped a piece of paper off and handed it to Hadi. "You're number seven. Find your number," he said pointing to the pile of clothing. "Your quarters have the same number."

Hadi had no idea what the number seven was or even what it meant, so he looked at the shape and tried to find the same shape on the pile of clothes. It took him a few minutes. To Hadi the number looked like two sticks or lines. He followed the other boys to the far end of the room. As he walked, he saw the man who had taken him talking with another man in a long white robe. Hadi saw them exchange money. With a quick bow, his captor dashed out a side door. Hadi never saw him again.

The boys walked single file through the camel souk. The smell here was different than at his home. It was a heavy, dirty smell of camels and manure. Hadi looked at the camels and then in their pens. He saw large clumps of brown dung everywhere. Flies swarmed around the camels' faces. It wasn't long before they were swarming around Hadi. He tried to hold his nose with one hand and swat the flies with his other. There were too many and Hadi nearly dropped his new clothes. A young boy behind him laughed. Hadi turned and scowled.

Lined up in front of the group of small shacks, the man with the turban gave directions. "Find your number and that is your room," he said. Hadi looked again at the piece of paper and looked at each building. Above the doors was a number. The boys scrambled to find their rooms and Hadi, just as anxious, looked carefully as he matched his number with one above the door. There, several doors down he saw the number seven and headed towards it. Much to his dismay, about ten other boys were headed in the same direction.

Hadi pushed his way inside. The room was hot and lined up against all the walls were dirty mattresses. Only a few blankets were visible but not enough for ten boys. Hadi ran to one on the far side, pushing other boys out of the way.

"Watch it!" one boy shouted.

Hadi didn't look back or say he was sorry. He had never slept on a mattress before. At home, his bed was a blanket on the hard ground. He shared another blanket with his five brothers and sisters and often woke in the night cold. Now, he had a bed of his own.

Hadi sat on his mattress and watched the other boys. They were all small in stature, had short black hair and dark skin, just like Hadi. He didn't recognize any of them. Some spoke in a language he didn't understand. Ten boys filled the room, *all from different parts of the world*, thought Hadi. He ran his dirty hand over the white, spotless shirts, cleaner than anything Hadi imagined could get clean. And not just one, but three! A pair of sandals was nestled in between the shirts. Hadi felt like a king. A new bed unlike any he had ever slept on and new clothes and shoes. The sheets and clothing were white as clouds and nearly as soft. Hadi was afraid to wear them for fear of getting them dirty. The other boys were undressing and slipping into their new clothes. Streaks of dirt and sweat marked the snow-white shirts but no one seemed to care.

Hadi slowly undressed, first taking off his shirt and then his pants. He rolled them up neatly and stuck them under his mattress. Taking the shirt on the top of his pile, he unfolded it and slipped it on. A cracked mirror hung on one wall and Hadi looked at his reflection. His dark eyes stared back as he smoothed his shirt out.

"I look like a girl," he moaned. The shirt covered his legs and touched the tips of his ankles.

Suddenly a man in a turban appeared in the door. "In Abu Dhabi you dress the way we want you to dress."

Hadi stood still and stared at the man. "Yes, sir," he said. All the boys quieted and watched as the man circled the room.

"It's time to eat," he bellowed and left. A sigh of relief filled the room. Hadi sat back down on the mattress. The boys filed out of the room, each one wearing a long shirt and looking a little like angels to Hadi. Hadi remembered the small rock he had stashed in his pocket. The rock from home, the only thing he brought with him. He pulled his pants back out and searched the pockets. Pulling out the brown sparkly lump Hadi wondered, *Where can I hide this?* Hadi looked around the room and decided it would be safe under his mattress in the corner. He lifted his long shirt so as not to get it dirty and kneeled on his mattress. He pushed his treasure into the corner. Knees dirty he ran out of the room to catch up with the other boys.

That night, the boys nestled into their mattresses. Hadi had eaten well and knew with a full stomach it might be easier to sleep. Hard as he tried, he couldn't. A young boy maybe five years old curled up in a ball and whimpered. Another young boy seven or eight kept saying over and over, "I want to go home, I want to go home."

Hadi tried to block out their cries. It was hard. Inside he was crying too. What were his parents doing? Were they trying to find him? Did they know what happened? He tossed and turned on the mattress and although it seemed to be more comfortable than sleeping on the dirt floor of his home, it wasn't. He didn't hear the familiar snores of his father or his little sister talking in her sleep. He wasn't as warm as he would be at home and he didn't feel safe.

The hut cold at night and camels, snorting and groaning outside, were unfamiliar to Hadi. As his eyes grew heavy, Hadi's last thoughts were of his family and how he would make it back home.

Chapter 3

The First Day

It can't be time already, Hadi thought as he rolled over to the sound of a ringing bell. *Clang-clang-clang,* it echoed across the yard and pierced Hadi's ears. He put his hands over them to block out the sound. The boys next to him scrambled to get up. They stood and stretched. Some folded the blankets while others pulled on their clothes. Hadi stood with them and dressed too.

"You better hurry," said one boy taller than Hadi with wavy black hair. "The master hates it when we're late for breakfast."

Hadi pulled on his long shirt, slipped his sandals over his feet and followed the other boys to the main building. The ground had cooled from the cold night and dew covered the few trees around the place. Hadi's mouth watered as the droplets caught the first morning light, the leaves glistening.

The boys quietly stood in front, kicking sand and looking about. The sun was just peaking over the desert horizon to the east and the last morning star glowed brightly, as if fighting the sun for one last turn in the sky. The great wooden doors, with intricate carvings on the big building, slowly opened and the boys rushed in.

Hadi followed the swarm of white shirts to a great room on the left side of the main hallway. There were rows of tables and benches beneath them and on top of the tables were plastic bowls of food and plastic cups filled with water. The boys clamored to find their seats and Hadi joined them.

Without saying a word to the boys next to him, Hadi devoured his food quickly. As soon as he had finished, another bell rang and the boys stood up and went back outside. There, a stately man dressed in a long white robe stood waiting. He had a white turban and a black beard as dark as night. His brown piercing eyes caught Hadi's as he passed by.

The boys stood in lines and the man began to call names. One by one the boys shouted, "Here!" When Hadi's name was called he quietly said, "Here." Looking down at the ground, Hadi saw a pair of fine leather shoes standing in front of him. He knew they belonged to the master.

"What's your name?" he asked pushing Hadi's face upward with his hand.

"Hadi."

"In my souk, when your name is called you shout, here! Only girls whisper quietly. Are you a girl?"

"No," said Hadi.

"You are new, aren't you?" asked the man.

"Yes," answered Hadi trying not to look him in the eyes. The man scared Hadi and he wished he would leave and move on to the next boy.

The man did back up a few steps. With a clear and loud voice he said, "My name is Master Aziz. This is what you will call me. I own this souk and therefore, I own you. You are in this country illegally, therefore you have no rights. If you try to escape, you will be thrown in jail. If you don't do your work, you will be punished. If you talk back to me or misbehave you will regret it. You have no family and this," he said raising his arms and circling them around in the air, "this, is your home."

A boy a few rows behind Hadi burst into tears. "I want to go home," he said.

Master Aziz pushed his way through the boys until he came to the one crying. He grabbed him by the arm and dragged him to the front. The young boy only four or five years old cried uncontrollably. His body shook and big round tears dropped to the ground leaving small dark circles in the dirt. Master Aziz slapped his face hard. Hadi jumped. The young boy immediately stopped crying and held his face.

"This is your home, boy. Cry again and you'll be sent there." Master Aziz pointed to a small building. It only had one wooden door, no windows and was smaller than a dog house.

"That's where you go when you get into trouble," whispered the boy next to Hadi. "It's hotter than a frying pan and you can barely lie down in it."

The young boy still in the grasp of Master Aziz, looked at the dog house and then back to Master Aziz. His body trembled and Hadi pleaded in his own mind, "Don't cry, don't cry."

The master let go of him. The boy ran back to his spot in line and didn't say another word. Everyone was quiet.

"I need all the new boys to stay here. The rest of you get to work." Master Aziz was joined by three older boys. He spoke to them quietly as if giving directions then he marched off to his house.

Hadi stuck close to the ten new boys. They were divided into three groups and brought to a small shack. The door was opened and inside, Hadi saw shovels and pitch forks. In the building next to that, there was hay and grain. One boy tossed Hadi a shovel. Each boy got something to clean with. Then they joined together at a corral.

Standing inside were tall camels, bigger than Hadi, bigger than the tallest man there. The camels were lazily eating the hay that was thrown on the ground. In one corner under an old olive tree was a long wooden trough. It was filled with water. Flies buzzed madly around the camels' heads, and the water trough. The camels twitched their ears but did little else to get the flies off. It smelled like manure and rotten eggs mixed together and brewed for several days.

"There, there and there," said one of the older boys pointing to big brown clumps in the dirt. "You will pick those up and put it here." He pointed to an old, wooden wheelbarrow parked on the outside of the fence. "Go! What are you waiting for?"

Hadi, along with the other boys, scurried to the clumps of manure. Flies squatted all over them and buzzed wildly as Hadi's shovel fast approached. He slid his shovel underneath one clump, picked it up and watched as half the pile fell off. Sighing, he quickly brought it to the wheelbarrow and maneuvered the shovel in between the wire fence. Turning the shovel, he dumped the manure in the wheelbarrow and went back to pick up what he had dropped. Once the corral was clean, they met again in the middle.

"Good," said the older boy pleased with their work. "Every day you must keep all of these corrals clean." He pointed behind him, beside him and in front of him.

Seeing many camels in each pen, he sighed deeply. *This is going to be a lot of work.*

As the morning went on, the sun rose higher in the sky. The air was stifling hot and Hadi, having nothing to eat or drink since breakfast felt miserable. As soon as the last corral was cleaned, they could eat lunch.

With dirty hands, Hadi again followed the boys to the dining room, ate and quickly left. Now, the camels had to be cleaned. Buckets, hoses brushes and combs were laid out in the shade under a group of trees. One by one, the camels were lead out of the corrals. Some camels fought hard with the boys, demanding not to go. They threw there heads in the air, groaned loudly and pulled back on the lead rope. Sometimes, the boys being so small were lifted into the air. Hadi learned quickly; the last thing you want to do is upset a camel!

As he tried to rescue one small boy, who was trying to lead a camel to the trees, Hadi grabbed hold of the lead rope. Suddenly, something wet and gooey hit him in the face. It smelled like vomit and Hadi thought he was going to throw up himself. He let go of the lead rope and the camel raced back into his corral.

Hadi wiped his face and looked at his hands. He smeared the goop on his shirt and raced to the trough to clean it off. The camel, with great aim, had spit at Hadi. As Hadi cleaned his face, he heard laughter behind him.

"Even the camels don't like you," someone said and the group of boys broke out into laughter.

Hadi stood up, grabbed a bucket of water and chased after the group of boys. He didn't know who teased him so he waved the bucket and splashed the nearest two. "One day it will be you that gets spit on!" he yelled and went back to retrieve the camel.

By the time all the camels were cleaned and brushed, they had made more messes in the corral. Hadi grabbed his shovel and again helped to clean the corrals. The sun was low in the sky and the air was cooling off. Dinner was near and Hadi could hardly wait. When the dinner bell rang, Hadi ran to the trough. Squatting on his knees, he washed his hands. As hard as he tried to scrub, not all the dirt came off.

"You better come or else they won't save dinner for you," said a small boy passing by. Hadi recognized him as the boy who laughed at him while he was standing in line. He stood up and followed him inside.

Not all was horrible at the souk. After dinner, the boys had some free time. They would play games, tell stories or sit and talk. Some would remain in the dining hall while others ventured outside into the yard. Hadi often joined the boys for a game of touch *wood*. Hadi knew the rules. It was like tag only you had to find some wood and touch it. You were safe as long as you were touching wood. Being in the desert, there was little wood. It was a challenge and didn't take long to be tagged *it*. The only wood the boys could find was the olive tree that stood in the yard near the camel's corrals, the big front doors on Master Aziz's house and the old wheelbarrow.

That night after dinner a game of *touch wood* was played. Hadi laughed as he chased three boys across the yard. They scrambled into the wheelbarrow, all trying to be safe. All Hadi had to do was tip them over and once one of them fell out, he could tag him! Hadi loved to play this game. It reminded him of playing with his brothers and sister. It was the only time he had a good laugh too and was able to forget about his life as a slave boy.

Day after day, Hadi and the boys cleaned corrals and camels. There was no change. The work was hard and Hadi developed calluses on his hands and feet. He had never worked so hard in his life and promised that when he returned home, he would never complain again about taking care of the chickens or his family.

Chapter 4

A New Friend

The nights were cool in the little souk in the desert. Because it was so hot during the day, Hadi couldn't wait for the sun to go down. But he knew later in the night he would awake, shivering because someone pulled the blanket off him. He splashed some water from the camel trough onto his face and looked at the sky. One by one, stars appeared and twinkled as if to say good night. His face dripping with water, Hadi moved to a date tree and sat at the base. He watched intently and counted each star as it appeared in the dark eastern sky. To his west, the last trail of golden pink darted across the horizon, then was gone.

Hadi felt his hopes plunge as quickly as the sun had disappeared.

"That's the same sky back home," he said quietly. He found the North Star easily and stared at it for a long time. *I wonder if Mama sees the same star*, he thought. He pushed the sand away with his feet and felt a tear drop from his eye.

Two months had passed and what did Hadi have to show for it? The boys were given a minuscule amount of money but Hadi didn't know why. They weren't allowed out of the souk. They couldn't go into the city or buy things. He saved his money in his pant pockets. It was his only hope. He would use the money one day to get back home.

He ate well enough and never felt hungry, yet he always felt an emptiness he couldn't fill with food, sleep or work. He looked at his hands. Dirt was embedded in every nail and groove. He couldn't even remember the last time he had bathed. Water was scarce and there weren't any rivers to jump in. Not like home. Hadi was never this dirty. A stream flowed by his house and Hadi would play in it with his brothers and sisters. He bathed often and there was always plenty of water. Hadi sighed. It had taken Hadi a few days to get used to the heat. It was different than in Multan. The heat was dry in the desert. In Multan it was heavy and wet. For days, Hadi craved water and drank from every source he could find. He even stole a few sips from the camel trough.

The souk was quiet that night. Some boys were still eating supper. Hadi had eaten quickly so he could get out into the fresh night air. The room where they all ate was hot and crowded and Hadi preferred to be left alone. Some boys were obnoxious, teasing Hadi each day about something. They stole Hadi's food, dropped a fly in it once and teased him. Hadi hated it all. He felt like everyone was laughing at him and couldn't make a friend. Of course, Hadi didn't try. Why they teased, he didn't know. Maybe because he was quiet and didn't join the boys in their jesting. Maybe because he rarely smiled or tried to make friends. He hated it at the souk and longed for home.

Each night was a struggle. Hadi had trouble sleeping at night all alone in his bed. The bed he could hardly believe was his in the beginning was now uncomfortable. *At home, I have many brothers and sisters to keep me warm,* he thought. My bed is too big here. Hadi longed to sleep on the floor and curl up next to someone, but didn't dare. Some nights Hadi would try to sleep on the floor. He dragged his blanket down and curled up into a ball. Each morning he awoke with a foot in his face and the boys laughing at him.

Laughter echoed from inside the dining room. Hadi looked back up at the stars. They shone so brightly across the sky now. The city was in the other direction, to the north and Hadi could see a glow on the horizon. Hadi lifted his arm and stretched his fingers as far as they could go. He thought maybe he could reach one of the stars, they seemed so close, but he couldn't reach any, and worst of all he couldn't reach his family whom he missed the most. If only he hadn't begged his mother to let him go to the market. If only he had appreciated his family more maybe he wouldn't be in this horrible place.

Hadi buried his head in his hands and cried. "I want to go home!"

He felt a tap on his shoulder. "You okay?" a timid voice reached out to him.

Hadi quickly wiped his tears with the sleeve of his shirt and looked up to see what person dared disturb him. He saw a young boy not much younger than him, maybe seven years old. His eyes were big and brown and his hair tasseled stood straight up in some places. Hadi couldn't help but give a little smile.

"Yeah, I'm okay. What do you want?"

"I just ate. I wanted to watch the stars," said the young boy. "But you're sitting in my spot."

"Your spot?" said Hadi. "How can it be your spot?"

"I always come here after I eat. I've never seen you here." The young boy sat down next to Hadi and leaned against the tree. "Want some dates?" He held out a handful of dried dates.

Hadi took some and popped them in his mouth. "Hey, you're the boy who laughed at me when I first got here," he said trying not to let any dates fall out.

"Yeah. You looked pretty funny trying to swat the flies and hang on to your new clothes!" The boy laughed. Hadi did not. He eyed him more closely and wasn't sure what it was he wanted. They sat together for a while and stared at the stars.

"Where you from?" asked the boy as he stared at the sky.

"A small village near Multan, in Pakistan," said Hadi. "Where are you from?"

"A small village in Bangladesh." The boy chewed loudly on a date.

"What's your name?" asked Hadi.

"Asim." He looked around the yard and kicked the dirt with the tip of his sandal. "What's your name?"

"I'm Hadi." He hung his head and wiped a fallen date off his shirt.

"Asim, how long have you been at the souk?"

Asim looked beyond Hadi as if her were trying to figure it out. "I don't know, Hadi. I've been here for years. I think they brought me over when I was three." Asim looked down at his hands and rubbed them together.

"Three years? Why that's nearly five years now. Why haven't you run away?" Hadi leaned closer to Asim so he could hear his answer.

Asim shrugged his shoulders. "You don't run away, Hadi. Besides, where would I go? I don't know who my family is anymore or where they are. I only know I'm from Bangladesh. I don't even know my last name."

"Your parents must be looking for you. Don't you want to go home?"

This is my home. If I run away, Master Aziz will hurt me. He threatens us all the time. I'm not supposed to be here, none of us are because we are illegals and we could go to jail, Hadi. We all could and I don't want to go there. They do bad things to you."

"What's an illegal?"

Asim sighed. "It means we're not here legally. The police and people like that don't want us here but they don't know what to do with us when they find us."

Hadi thought about this. He was truly a stranger in this country. He couldn't speak their language, he wasn't sure how to get home and Master Aziz and his guards were mean. Everyone was mean!

Hadi spoke up. "Asim, I am going home. I am getting out of here as soon as I can and you're coming with me."

Looking up at the sky, Asim smiled. "I would love to go with you, Hadi but I can't. All I know is life here. I eat well, have a bed, clothes and even get some money. What would I do out there all by myself?" Asim pointed towards the road.

Hadi looked at Asim. "You're a slave here. No one cares about you or me or anyone else. You can come home and live with my family."

The two boys sat in silence a little longer then Asim spoke up. "Do you miss your home?"

Hadi felt like he might cry again if he said he did, but he wasn't so sure Asim missed his home. Did Asim even remember what his home and family was like? "I do," said Hadi.

"I know," said Asim nodding. "When I first got here all I could think about was my family. I would see there faces everywhere and even heard their voices. I don't know. It's like time has killed those memories. Sometimes, I think they were just a dream."

Hadi leaned against the tree and hung his head. He couldn't imagine ever forgetting his family. He loved them too much. Even when his mother told him to do chores, or when he had to watch his little sister, or even when he had to go to the market, he still loved them. What he wouldn't do now to be working at home instead of the stinky camel farm. Hadi looked at the corral of camels. Their long mouths slowly opened and closed as they ate the hay. Some stood in the corner watching Hadi and Asim, letting out a groan every now and then as if they were a part of the conversation.

"Have you ridden a camel yet?" asked Hadi. He had heard talk that some of the boys would get to learn to ride camels and race them.

"I rode one a few days ago. Master Aziz said he was going to start training me before I started to grow."

"You are so lucky," said Hadi. He wiggled his toes and shook some sand off them. A rush of energy returned to his body. He wanted to know more about camel racing. "I've been here for two months and the closest I've gotten to a camel is shoveling its poop."

"I've been here almost five years, Hadi, and I'm just starting to ride. Maybe you should wait a while. It will happen." Both boys looked to the sky as if the stars held all the answers.

"I'm tired of working. I hate it here and I miss my family." Hadi heard the other boys and men laughing again. He shook his head in disbelief. How could they be so happy? They were stolen from their homes too.

"I miss my family. Maybe I could be a part of yours some day," said Asim. He scratched his head and spit in the dirt. "I always have sand in my mouth."

Hadi laughed. So did he.

"Tomorrow, I will ask Master Aziz if you can start riding, you know before you get too big," said Asim. He elbowed Hadi and giggled. "You're already big, if you ask me."

"Am not!" shouted Hadi. "I'm small. Small for my age. Stand up and let's see how much taller I am than you."

The two boys quickly jumped up and stood back to back. Hadi ran his hand over his head and then down a little to feel where Asim's head was. "See, you're not much smaller than me. How old are you?"

"Eight," said Asim.

"Ha! I'm nine and still as small as you! By the time you're my age you'll be a giant!"

"You can't ride a camel as well as me," said Asim. He smiled proudly and folded his arms in front of him.

"Can too!" said Hadi. "I promise I'll be the best camel jockey in the Middle East and then I will get to go home!"

"I promise I will be," said Asim. He nudged Hadi. Hadi pushed him back. Asim jumped on Hadi and tackled him to the ground, laughing.

"See I'm stronger than you," said Asim.

"Are not!"

The two rolled around in the sand laughing. It was the most fun Hadi had had since he arrived at the camel souk. Exhausted, Hadi rolled off Asim and lay on his back. The moon, not nearly full, inched its way up the black veil of the sky. Hadi hadn't thought much about racing camels. No one had said he could. Now there was a chance. His heart raced at the idea. Hadi imagined himself covered in beautiful silk ribbons, crowds cheering his name, "Hadi! Hadi*!" Maybe I'll be on TV*, he dreamed. Asim's elbow jabbed him in the ribs.

"I'll be your friend, if you'll be mine," said Asim.

Hadi turned and smiled. "Alright."

Asim sat up on his arms and punched Hadi in the gut.

"Let's not tell anyone about how much we miss our mother's though, okay?" said Hadi.

"Deal."

"Hadi! Asim!" shouted an angry man's voice. "Get to your rooms at once or else!"

"We have to go," said Hadi. "See you tomorrow." Hadi quickly got up and ran towards his room. He looked back to see Asim slowly get up and shake the sand from his shirt.

"Goodnight friend," whispered Hadi.

Chapter 5

Master Aziz and the Stranger

The next morning was the same as every other morning at the souk. Hadi rose and dressed in a clean, long, white shirt. He looked in the cracked mirror hanging on the wall, spit in his hand and flattened his as hair best he could. He opened his mouth wide and looked inside. One of his teeth had fallen out, but he wouldn't be getting a new one. The one that fell out was his adult tooth. He splashed water on his face and washed his hands. He looked at the boys still sound asleep before slipping out.

Hadi crept in the early morning hours to the dining room for breakfast. On the other side of the room he saw Asim already seated at a long table eating his breakfast. Hadi quickly rushed over.

"Did you get into trouble?" Asim asked as Hadi sat down.

"No." Another young boy brought a bowl filled with cous cous and handed it to Hadi. He stuck two fingers in and scooped up the tasty pasta, shoveling it into his mouth. It tasted good.

"Good thing," said Asim ripping off a piece of bread from the loaf that sat in the middle of the table.

Hadi looked around as other boys entered the dining room. Then he looked back at Asim. "Are you going to talk to Master Aziz today?"

Asim shrugged. "I'll try but I can't promise anything. He's not an easy man to talk to."

"I know. All I want to do is race camels. That's the only way I'm going to get out of here." He had to keep hope that his life wouldn't be spent enslaved at a camel souk.

The sun slowly crept up from behind the horizon and cast its first rays through the narrow windows of the dining room. Hadi finished his breakfast and followed Asim out the door. The sun already felt hot on Hadi's head. He grabbed a shovel and began cleaning the corrals.

~   ~   ~

Five hours later, Hadi noticed the sun high in the sky. Sweat dripped off his brow and his throat was dried out. He had just finished cleaning his last corral when he saw a large, white car race down the dusty road. Hadi watched the car pull up to the main building, the one where Master Aziz lived. The driver jumped out and rushed to the other side to open the door. Slowly a tall man exited the car. He straightened his robes and looked around the souk. His bearded face was stern and serious as if he were there to do business. He was dressed in the finest clothes. Hadi noticed a bright sparkle on the man's wrist. *Gold*, thought Hadi. He looked down at his own bare arms, covered in dirt and dung, not gold. Hadi watched the man intently. *What is his business I wonder?*

"Hadi. Get to work. Don't let Master see you standing there," said Asim under his breath.

Hadi took his shovel and pretended to dig. His stomach told him it was time to eat. He wished he could join the strange, rich man for lunch. Then, he surely would eat like a king!

Master Aziz rushed out of the building and bowed several times. He too wore his finest clothes. Hadi listened as he raked some hay in the corner. A large loping camel approached. He nuzzled Hadi's leg, groaned and grabbed a mouthful of hay.

"Good day," said Master Aziz.

"Good day to you," said the stranger.

Master Aziz raised his arms and proudly exclaimed, "Welcome." The kingly looking man laughed and then walked inside the building. Master Aziz followed beckoning workers to attend to the guest's every need.

Hadi wanted to know what they were going to talk about. His work was finished and he had some time before lunch. The older boy who was in charge of Hadi was busy talking with his friends. They stood on the other side of the corral.

"I'm done here," he shouted to him. The boy just waved and nodded. Hadi put the shovel against a tree and walked past the driver, who sat asleep in the car. Quickly he dashed around to the side of the building. Slinking like a lizard along the wall of the building, Hadi stopped briefly to listen to voices. When he heard Master Aziz, he looked around him one last time to make sure no one was near. At the end of the building was a long wooden fence. Hadi couldn't run that way if he was caught but at the bottom near the ground was a small hole in the wire and wooden planks. *I might be able to squeeze through that*, he thought. Voices drifted out the window above his head. He had found the room the guest and Master Aziz were in. He could hear the voices inside and he wanted to see what they were doing. Pushing an old bucket under the window, Hadi carefully climbed it and peered in.

From here, he could see the guest and Master Aziz clearly. They were seated on the floor, which was covered in colorful Persian rugs. In front of them was a coffee set and Master Aziz poured coffee into two brass cups. The guest tilted his cup back and forth to let Master Aziz know that he had enough. Then Master Aziz filled his own cup. They sat quietly and sipped their coffee. A young boy brought in bowls of food and placed them in front of the men. Hadi's stomach growled loudly. Raw vegetables, some stuffed with rice, roasted lamb, olives, bowls of steaming hot rice and cous cous and Matzoh adorned the table. *If only I could eat like that,* Hadi thought and rubbed his tummy. He watched the two men eat. As they stuffed food in their mouths, they talked.

"You know, Aziz, you have very good camels, but you charge too much," said the guest. He leaned back on a pillow and rubbed his full, round belly. Master Aziz scowled and leaned back against another pillow. He crossed his arms. "I can only give you 1000 dirham for each camel." The guest pulled out a velvet purse and hesitantly opened it. Hadi watched from the window leaning his body against the side of the building so he wouldn't fall.

"What do you mean, only 1000? My camels are worth three times as much." Hadi reached for the window sill and kicked the side of the wall as he tried to pull himself up to get a better look.

"Humph. Some of your camels are old. I could only race them another year," shouted the guest.

Hadi's heart raced. The sun warmed his face. He wiped his brow and peeked through the window. This time Master Aziz stood and paced across the rugs. Then he came right over to the window where Hadi was. Hadi ducked low, being careful not to fall off the bucket. It was hard and the bucket wobbled under his feet.

"I will sell you my camels for 2000 dirham. They are worth that much just for their skins." Master Aziz turned and faced his guest.

Hadi heard the guest laugh. It echoed throughout the room in a low thunderous rumble. "You are a true business man, Aziz. I like that. 1500 dirham and that is my final offer."

"Argh," snarled Master Aziz. He kicked the wall. "1500 dirham and no less!"

Master Aziz walked away from the window. Hadi stood up, his back aching from being hunched over, and peered inside.

The stranger pulled out many dirhams from a leather wallet and handed them to Master Aziz. He counted each one carefully. "It is all there, Aziz. Don't you trust me?"

Master Aziz carefully eyed his money. "Tomorrow you come with your trucks and you can take five camels."

"My men will be here first thing in the morning, Aziz." The guest stood and stretched. Master Aziz showed him the door and together they walked out. Hadi heard two car doors slam and then the engine whirring as it sped off back down the road. He sat on the bucket, his stomach growled loudly.

"You boy," said Master Aziz. Hadi jumped up and looked at him. He was standing by the window and staring down at Hadi. His black eyebrows were pointed upward like arrows and his finger waved back and forth. He pointed a long, skinny finger right at Hadi. Master Aziz's face crinkled and the veins in his head bulged out. "You come here."

Hadi obeyed. His heart raced and suddenly his adventure was over. He was caught! Ashamed that he had spied on Master Aziz, he walked to the front door and through the building to the room where Master Aziz was. He folded his hands in front of him and looked at the ground.

"Do you always spy on your master?" asked Master Aziz.

"No sir," said Hadi, still refusing to look up.

"What were you doing, boy?" Master Aziz sat back down at the table.

"I wanted to learn about the camels, how you sell them and race them." Hadi stood still. He was afraid to move in front of such a powerful man.

"It is not right for you to spy. Besides you missed your lunch. Now you won't work well."

Hadi felt Master Aziz's eyes on him. "Where are you from?"

"Multan, in Pakistan."

"I know where Multan is," interrupted Master Aziz. "I've been there. What's your name?" Grabbing an olive, Master Aziz popped it into his mouth.

"Hadi." He crossed his arms in front of him trying to hold his stomach and keep it from rumbling. Now the hunger pangs hit him like a rock. He eyed a bowl of lamb still sitting on the table. A big, black fly flew from one plate to another.

"Did you come here to race camels, Hadi? Or clean their pens?"

Hadi thought about this for a moment. He didn't choose to come here. He was kidnapped. Anger swelled inside and Hadi felt his face grow hot. Before he knew what was happening he blurted out, "I did not choose to be here, sir. You kidnapped me. You took me away from my family and all that I know!" Hadi's eyes stung as the first tears dribbled down his cheek. He quickly wiped the tears with the back of his hand. Master Aziz stared at him.

"I did not kidnap you, Hadi. You were brought to me. I don't know where most of the boys come from and I don't ask. I need workers and I need young, small boys to race camels." Master Aziz picked up another olive and turned it in his fingers. Then he tossed it to Hadi. "Eat it, Hadi. I can tell you are hungry."

Hadi caught the olive and took a small bite out of it.

"Chances are, Hadi, your family has forgotten you and no one cares anymore. This is your home now and the sooner you accept that fact, the happier you will be."

Hadi wanted to scream. *I will never accept that*, he thought. *My family loves me and misses me.* Hadi hung his head. He had already said too much to Master Aziz and he learned the hard way with his mother, that he couldn't argue with an adult. It never worked. He never got his way. Instead, he resolved to make a plan, a plan for his escape.

"So, Hadi. Let me ask you again. Do you want to race camels or clean their pens?" Master Aziz forked a piece of lamb and bit a chunk off. Juice ran down his beard and Hadi watched as it dripped onto his finely sewn clothes.

"Race, sir. I want to race."

"You know it is very dangerous." Master Aziz grabbed a handful of dates.

"Yes, sir. I know I'd be good."

"You do? How?"

"Because I have to be the best. I've wanted to be a camel jockey for a long time, sir." Hadi lied. He never even knew about the camel jockeys until Asim told him. He knew it was the only way he would get home.

"Hadi sit down." Hadi did as he was told. He stared at the remaining food. "Eat, boy. Otherwise you are no good to me."

Hadi reached out with his right hand and grabbed a piece of lamb. Master Aziz rang a bell and the young boy who had served them before returned.

"Fetch me some water, for the boy."

The young boy bowed and left.

A jug of water was placed in front of Hadi and he drank it so fast he got the hiccups. Since he got to Abu Dhabi, his throat and mouth never felt quenched. Hadi wiped the drips from his mouth and stood up.

"Thank you, Master Aziz. You have been very kind. May I go?"

Master Aziz stopped him.

"Asim also tells me you wish to ride camels. You and Asim, are you good friends?"

Hadi smiled. It had been a long time since he had a good friend. "Yes, sir."

"Tomorrow morning after breakfast you and Asim meet me at the south pen. You will learn first by watching."

"Thank you." He looked at Master Aziz and bowed. "Thank you, sir."

"Go, Hadi and prepare for your training."

Hadi rushed out to tell Asim the good news.

~ ~ ~

"Asim!" shouted Hadi as he raced across the dirt driveway. An older worker stopped him and grabbed his arm.

"Why aren't you working, boy!" he shouted.

Hadi stopped short. Out of breath Hadi could barely speak. "I was talking with Master Aziz. I have good news."

The older boy, probably close to fourteen years and much taller than Hadi crossed his arms and glared. "Well. I don't have all day. Tell me the good news first."

Excited about his news he couldn't wait to tell someone. "Master Aziz is going to teach me to be a camel jockey." Hadi stood looking at the boy with a smile so wide and proud; he felt his face might burst in half. The boy continued to stare at Hadi without the slightest smile for his happiness.

"Don't get your hopes up. You are bigger than most of the boys who become camel jockeys. Besides, he's just lying to you." The boy turned and walked into the pen where he shoveled up camel dung and tossed it into a wheel barrow.

Hadi felt the heat in his body rise. He clenched his fist and took a step to go after the boy. "He is not a liar!" shouted Hadi. Anger rose from his toes and swelled to his head. Gritting his teeth, Hadi turned and ran as fast as he could, across the dirt road and out onto the main road. He kept running until he couldn't breathe and collapsed on the side of the road. It was hot and burned his back, but he didn't care. He lay there looking up at the sky, the cloudless sky and the hot sun.

"Cook me and be done with me!" said Hadi in a parched voice. He didn't really want to die. He wanted to go home. He wanted to be with his family, with people who loved him.

A car drove by, slowed then backed up until it was a few feet in front of Hadi. A man jumped out and ran over to Hadi who lay motionless on the faded asphalt.

"I think he's dead!" shouted the man to someone in the car. Hadi heard a car door open, then shut and the light footsteps of a second person. Dressed in black, with only her eyes showing, a woman bent over and touched Hadi's wrist. She smiled at him then lifted his head and poured some water into his mouth.

"Mama?" whispered Hadi.

"No," said the woman. She helped Hadi to his feet.

"Can you take me with you?" he asked looking behind him down the road. Maybe this was his chance to escape. "Please take me with you!"

The man handed Hadi the water bottle. "Where do you belong?" he asked.

Hadi didn't hesitate. He knew where he belonged and it wasn't in Abu Dhabi or a camel souk. "I belong in Pakistan with my family. Can you take me there?"

The man looked down the road. "Did you come from the souk?" he asked pointing in the direction of Master Aziz's souk.

Hadi looked. What should he say? Should he tell him yes? Will they understand that he was kidnapped and brought there against his will? Should he lie? He couldn't think fast enough.

"Get in the car," said the man. He opened a back door for Hadi. *This is it*, Hadi thought. *I'm saved!* The woman got in the front. Hadi felt a rush of cool air blow across his face and through his hair. He ran his hands along the leather seats and sat back relaxed. He was so excited all he could think about was his family and how he would be seeing them shortly. Then something terribly wrong happened. The car headed straight for the camel souk and turned down the dusty driveway.

"No!" shouted Hadi. "I can't stay here. I want to go home. Please turn the car around."

The man driving the car looked in his rearview mirror at Hadi. His eyes told Hadi that he wished he could help but his mouth said something very different. "I can't, boy. I found you and so I must return you to your master, Master Aziz. He is a very powerful man and if he finds out I helped one of his boys escape, my family and I will be in great danger. Please understand, child. I can't."

As the car pulled up to Master Aziz's house, Hadi saw two men come out of the building. The car came to a stop and the man got out. He opened the back door and beckoned Hadi to come out. "I can't go back," he whispered yet knew he had no choice. He slid along the cool leather seat and out the door.

"What is going on here?" asked Master Aziz as he raced from the front door. "Hadi, what did you do?"

Hadi said nothing. He listened to the man tell how he found Hadi lying in the road and brought him back.

"You did a good job," said Master Aziz. "Thank you."

Master Aziz pulled Hadi by the arm and brought him into the house. Hadi trembled when he saw Master Aziz pull a whip used for camel racing off a nearby table. "No, Master," begged Hadi. "I am sorry. I'll never run away again."

"This is your home now, Hadi. I told you before. And just like a parent disciplining a child, so must I discipline you. Turn around."

Hadi slowly turned and faced the wall. He had never been whipped, not by his parents not by anyone. Suddenly, the crack of the whip pierced the air and Hadi doubled over in pain. The whip struck his lower back not once but twice. Hadi fell against the wall crying.

"This should teach you to never betray me again, Hadi. If you want to race camels, you must obey the rules here. There is no where for you to go beyond my fences. It is hot and the desert stretches for miles."

Hadi slowly turned around and looked Master Aziz in the eyes. "I will not betray you, Master." Hadi had lied again for as those words shot out of his mouth he resolved to run away for good. If it meant he had to lie to the master then he would do whatever it would take to get back home. *No one should be a slave.*

"Good," said Master Aziz. "Go back to your room and rest. We have a busy day tomorrow."

Hadi walked out of the building and never looked back.

Chapter 6

Training

The next morning, Hadi's back stung with pain. As he rolled off the mattress, he noticed a blood stain. Soon it would fade like so many of the stains on the mattress. His back was sore and it was hard to dress. He slowly made his way with the other boys to breakfast, ate and walked back outside into the morning sun. Today he was going to start his training. He was excited, even if he could hardly walk.

"Come here boy, I need to talk to you," said Master Aziz. Hadi turned around. He had not seen anyone. The low voice scared him. Hadi smoothed his rumpled black hair and wiped the beads of sweat from his temples.

"Today is your day, Hadi. Today you learn to ride camels." Master Aziz walked passed Hadi straight for the corral. Hadi followed closely behind him skipping to keep up. *Race camels*, he thought. *I'm going to be a camel jockey!*

Hadi's spirits rose and he smiled. Master Aziz climbed between the wire fences and walked over to a very small, timid looking camel. Hadi was sure she winked at him. Already in the corral, Asim was saddling his camel. He nodded to Hadi.

"This one will be yours for practice. She is only a year old, not fully grown yet. If you do well, maybe you can race in the big race. However!" shouted Master Aziz. "You have to get that smile off your face or else you'll make the camels nervous."

Hadi nodded and pinched his lips together tightly. He had never ridden a camel. *How difficult can it be?* he thought.

"No smiles!" warned Master Aziz. "Follow Asim and me."

They walked past the big building to an area Hadi had never seen. Behind the building was a small racetrack. On one side were some bleachers. Hadi looked beyond the track. He saw only the brown desert sand for miles beyond. Two camels jogged around the track and the boys on top of them were yelling loudly. They were young boys and their yells were high-pitched. Hadi covered his ears. The camels were making a horrid noise—a low guttural sound that came from their bellies. He sat on the bleachers behind three boys younger than he. They elbowed each other and giggled as they looked at Hadi.

"What's so funny?" Hadi asked.

"You are too big to ride," chided one boy. He was missing his two front teeth and Hadi noticed he spit a little when he talked.

"Am not!" said Hadi.

"Are too. How old are you, twelve?" asked one.

"I'm ten," said Hadi.

"Too old," said the third boy. "You're done for."

"What do you mean?" Hadi turned and faced the boys. They giggled and huddled together. Then one spoke up. "After you turn twelve some boys are let go. The master sends them away."

"Sometimes the master kills them too," said another.

"I don't believe that. Master Aziz would never kill anyone." Hadi's voice trembled. He remembered being whipped by him and suddenly he wasn't so sure.

"Doesn't matter much anyway. You don't have long either way." The boys giggled again.

The boys turned to watch the camels and snickered under their breath.

Hadi wanted to go back. Training now seemed hopeless.

"You better stash some of your money so no one can take it," said the youngest boy turning around so he faced Hadi directly. "You don't have much time left."

"Stop saying that!" shouted Hadi. "Besides, the same thing will happen to you."

"Nope. We are planning ahead. We hide some of our money. We will run away before the master can kill us."

"You got it all figured out do you?" asked Hadi. He gripped his sweaty hands together and rubbed them. He couldn't wait to get back to his room and check under his mattress.

"Hadi, pay attention!" shouted Master Aziz. He whipped the camel with a long thin stick. Asim, tied on to the saddle, screamed and the camel went into a full, wobbly gallop. Asim looked like he was about to fall off. The camel bounced and groaned. Asim looked more like a rag doll than a little boy. Master Aziz snapped the whip again. Hadi jumped at the sound of the crack and the boys around him giggled.

Then they moved away, whispering in each other's ears and looking at Hadi. He didn't care. He had more important things to worry about like where his money was and when he was going to learn to ride. He threw a towel over his head to block the sun. There was no shade and it was August. Hadi felt sand in his mouth but had no idea how it got there. It didn't really matter; there was always sand somewhere on his body. If it wasn't his mouth, it was his nose or ears and between his toes. He spit and watched as the saliva landed on the bleacher. Poof! It was gone in a second, evaporated by the hot sun.

Master Aziz walked the camel over to Hadi with Asim still on its back. "Did you watch, Hadi?" he asked. He pulled a small towel from his robe and wiped his brow.

Hadi nodded. He was too tired from the sun to speak. Hadi looked up at Asim. He sat slumped over, his eyes glassy and staring into space. He looked straight at Hadi, his big brown eyes dazed. *Poor, Asim. He looks so tired,* thought Hadi.

"Maybe tomorrow you will ride," said Master Aziz. "Take this camel and Asim back to the souk. Don't forget to water the camel and give her grain. She needs it to keep up her strength." Master Aziz patted the camel on its neck.

Hadi grabbed hold of the reins and pulled. The camel towered over him as the top of Hadi's head only came up to her shoulder. The camel pulled back on the reins and groaned. She didn't want to go anywhere. Hadi pulled harder. The camel retaliated and lifted Hadi off his feet. Master Aziz cracked his whip on the animal's rump. "Show her who is boss, Hadi," he said. She stepped quickly, nearly knocking Hadi over. Hadi watched as Master Aziz marched back to his house. The camel obediently followed. As soon as they got back, Hadi led the camel to her corral. "Asim, you okay?" he asked.

Asim nodded his head but remained motionless.

"Let me help you down." Hadi stood on a trough so he was almost as tall as the camel and untied the rope that held Asim to the saddle. He grabbed Asim by the waist and helped him off. "That was some ride," said Hadi.

"All that bouncing hurts my head," said Asim. "I don't feel so well."

"You sit over there and I'll get you some water," said Hadi pointing to their favorite olive tree. Remembering how his mother took care of him when he didn't feel well, Hadi went to fetch the hose and dragged it to the corral. He held it up to Asim's mouth. A cool trickle of water slowly dribbled out of the hose and then it stopped all together. Hadi looked behind him to see what the hose was caught on or where it was crimped.

"Hadi, you disobey me you will live to regret it," said Master Aziz. He had crimped the hose in his hand so the water wouldn't flow. "Camels get taken care of first."

"But Asim doesn't feel well," Hadi said standing up.

"Asim is fine. The camels come first." Master Aziz yanked the hose hard and pulled it out of Hadi's hands.

"Yes, sir." He picked the hose up and raced it over to the camel trough and filled it. *If I hurry here, I can help Asim*, Hadi thought as he watched the water flow into the trough. Two camels meandered over and sipped the water through their mouths like a straw. Master Aziz watched him the entire time. Hadi went to the barn and retrieved a bucket of the high protein grain. He fed it to the camel, which immediately threw it up.

Master Aziz laughed. "That's a good sign, Hadi, when the camel throws up. Means she's going to win." Hadi nodded then got some hay and spread it out. Hadi watched as Master Aziz walked into the building.

Hadi raced to Asim with the hose and let him drink. "Thank you, Hadi," Asim said in a raspy voice. He was protected from the sun yet even in the shade it was blistering hot.

"You don't look so well," said Hadi.

"I'm just tired."

"You go lie down and I will do your chores too," said Hadi. Asim nodded and walked slowly to his room.

Hadi walked back to the corral and kicked a bucket. He watched it fly then hit the ground and roll a bit further. "I hate this place," he mumbled. He picked up a shovel and scooped up the manure. Shovel by shovel he flung it into the wheelbarrow. Sometimes he missed, other times it landed in with a thump. On his last throw his shovel whacked the neck of a camel standing nearby. Before Hadi could see if he was okay, a wad of sticky, smelly spit landed on the side of Hadi's face. Hadi looked at the camel and wiped the spit and sweat off his brow.

"You stupid beast!" he shouted. He slammed the shovel down and took the manure to the manure pile. He wanted to scream as loud as he could. Instead, he faced the east, the direction he had come on that horrible night when he was taken from his home. His mother's face flashed in his mind, then his father's face and each of his brothers and sister. After he saw the treatment the camels received compared to him or Asim, he was more determined than ever to go home.

~   ~   ~

When he finished both his and Asim's chores, he quickly went to Asim's room. *I hope he is okay*, thought Hadi. He came to the doorway and pushed the blanket aside. It was dark with only a little light shining between the blanket and the door frame. Hadi saw Asim lying on his mattress in the corner. Sweat bubbled on his brow and dripped down the side of his face. Hadi saw streaks of dirt on his cheeks and knew he had been crying. With a weak smile, Asim looked at Hadi and whispered, "What are you doing here?"

"I finished our chores and wanted to see how you were doing?" Hadi kneeled beside him and stared. "Are you okay?"

"Sort of. I don't know. I don't feel so well. I'm really hot."

Hadi pulled the blanket of his legs. "It's pretty hot in here. Why do you have a blanket on you?"

"I was cold before." Asim pulled his arms to his chest and shivered. "I'm cold again."

"You don't look so good, Asim. Maybe I should get the master." Hadi got up on his knees.

"No! Don't go. Just stay here and talk to me. Tell me about our run away plans and how I will live with you and your family, Hadi." Asim shot another slight smile and touched his arm.

"Okay. Well, I haven't made plans yet really, but I do have some ideas," Hadi began. "I'm thinking we'll have to do it at night though, when everyone is asleep."

"Yeah, that's probably a good idea. How will we get out? The front gate is locked at night and we can't climb over the barb-wire fence."

Hadi thought about this a moment. "Good point, Asim. I think I found a hole in the fence when I was spying on Master Aziz the other day. It's behind his house and he doesn't even know it!" Hadi laughed at his discovery. "You might be too big to fit through it," he joked.

"You're bigger than me," said Asim.

"Am not!" argued Hadi. "Stand up and we'll measure ourselves again. I'm sure you grew a few inches since the other day."

Asim rolled his head to one side. "I can't get up, Hadi. It hurts too much." He held his stomach and his body trembled. "Can you pull the blanket back up, Hadi."

Hadi reached over and pulled the scratchy woolen blanket to Asim's waist. "I have to get you some help," said Hadi. "Do you something to eat? Drink?"

Asim's smile was weaker than before. "I just want to sleep." He rolled to the wall and curled up in a ball. Hadi sat there a moment unsure of what to do. He didn't want to leave his friend but he couldn't stay there either. The other boys would be coming back from their chores or dinner soon. He stood up and headed for the door.

"Hadi," Asim spoke quietly.

"Yeah."

"If I'm going to be a part of your family, do you think your parents will love me like a son? Like you?"

Hadi didn't hesitate. He knew his mother and father would take him in as one of their own. "Of course, Asim. They'd love you like a son."

Asim shivered and closed his eyes. Hadi turned and walked outside. The setting sun glared at him as if it were angry. Red and pink streaks lit the clouds and reminded Hadi of the brightly colored clothing at his village back home. Hadi was mad; his friend was sick and there was nothing he could do for him. Unless he could escape with Asim and give him a home he always dreamed of. Excitement raced through Hadi like a bolt of lighting. He had to get out of there not just for him, but for Asim too. His stomach growled angrily wanting food and Hadi raced to dinner.

Chapter 7

Hadi's Turn

That night after Hadi ate his dinner he checked on Asim. Many of his roommates were still eating. A few gathered outside for a game of touch wood, but Hadi had other plants. Asim hadn't shown up to eat and Hadi was worried. It was quieter than usual at the camel souk, which meant that Hadi had to be extra careful not to make any noise. He crept along the side of the buildings like a mouse hiding from a cat. He sneaked from one shadow to another, until he came to Asim's room.

"Asim," he whispered loudly. There was no answer. He peered in one of the windows. It was dark inside. *Maybe he's still eating,* thought Hadi. *And I just didn't see him.* To make sure Asim wasn't in the room, he rapped gently on the door, then jumped to the side and hid in the shadows. He heard someone moan, and then the door opened slowly. Hadi couldn't see who it was. He quietly whispered, "Asim."

"Who's there?" asked a strange voice. Then the voice turned into a man who peered directly at Hadi. "What do you want, boy?"

"I'm sorry, sir. I was looking for Asim." Hadi's legs felt a little weak. He wanted to run back to his room yet he was too worried about Asim to leave.

"Asim? Oh you mean the young boy who was in this room. He's gone," said the man.

"What do you mean he's gone?" asked Hadi peering into the building.

"Don't know. They came and got him earlier. Took all his things too. Told me he wasn't coming back. There's a new boy coming in tomorrow."

Hadi ran back to his room. Confused, he sat on his mattress and thought hard. "Where can he be?" he said over and over. Were the boys on the stands right? Did they take Asim away because he was no good to the souk? To Master Aziz? Was he really ill? Maybe they sent him home to be with his family. Who will be my friend? Hadi felt the tears start to swell. "You're not going to cry," he told himself. "Only babies cry and you're not a baby!" He wiped the tears. Then he remembered his money. He pulled the mattress back and found a small wad of bills and coins. At least it was still there. Hadi quickly put the mattress back down over it and sighed.

Footsteps outside came closer to the room. Suddenly the cloth that was the door was pushed aside and one of his roommates stood in the doorway holding an oil lantern. "Hadi, what are you doing all alone in the dark?" he asked.

"Nothing," said Hadi kicking the ground with his bare foot.

"Do you want me to leave this with you?" asked the boy pointing to his lantern.

"No," said Hadi. "Do you know what happened to Asim?" He sat up hoping that his roommate would know.

"Oh yeah. Asim got sick. He couldn't walk or anything. I heard them talk at dinner he might have a head problem. They took him to a hospital."

"Did you hear anything else? Is he coming back?" Hadi asked hoping the answer would be yes!

"I doubt it. Boys never come back when they are that sick. You want this or what?"

Hadi shook his head. *Poor Asim.* The boy left, the light from his lantern following him. Hadi rolled over on his side and faced the rough wall.

All Hadi could think about was his family. Were they seeing *any* of the money he was making? Hadi knew now that he had to save as much as he could and then run away. He had to go back home. He grabbed his precious rock sitting undisturbed under the corner of his mattress. He felt the grooves and ridges and remembered the road where he found it. It reminded him of the green fields and rivers frothing over with water. He remembered his mother rubbing his head and telling him how she loved him. Hadi sighed and breathed deep. The cool air filled his lungs and it hurt as he breathed in deeply. A shiver ran through his body. Wrapping his arms around himself for warmth, Hadi fell asleep.

~   ~   ~

The next morning was no different than the rest. It was already hot. The boys and men were either stirring in their rooms or finishing breakfast. Hadi was one of them. He walked to the corral where Master Aziz stood waiting. He did not hesitate and completely forgot his place at the souk—his low, demeaning place, which put him on the level of a worm.

"Where is Asim?" Hadi demanded.

Master Aziz shrugged his shoulders. He grabbed the reins and led the camel out of his corral. "Asim is gone. Don't ask questions, Hadi. Mind your own business."

"Gone? Do you mean dead?" asked Hadi. He had to know what happened to his young friend.

Master Aziz laughed.

"Tell me! I need to know." Hadi grabbed Master Aziz's sleeve.

Master Aziz whipped around and glared at Hadi. "I am your master!" he shouted. Don't ever touch me or talk to me in that manner."

Hadi backed away. "I-I'm sorry," he said. Then he started to cry. "I want to know if Asim is dead."

Master Aziz walked towards Hadi. "I like you, boy. For this I will tell you. Asim was very sick and sent to a hospital in Abu Dhabi. He died earlier this morning." Master Aziz turned and began walking towards the race track. Hadi had his answer though it was not what he wanted to hear. His head dropped and the pit of his stomach ached like he had eaten poison. Not Asim!

He followed his master to the same place they were at the day before. The two other boys weren't there today. Hadi took a deep breath. He was relieved there weren't any spectators. Master Aziz made the camel lie down so he could climb on top. "Since Asim is gone, you will take his place. I'll show you some things, and then you can try." He led the camel to the middle of the dusty track. Hadi tried to pay attention but Asim, kept popping into his head.

"Hey, you riding today?" came a voice from behind. Hadi turned only to find the same boys that were there yesterday. He didn't say anything and turned back to watch Master Aziz.

"What a jerk. He won't even talk to us."

Hadi focused on his master, squinting his eyes so he could see. Master Aziz on top of his camel, raced around the track once and walked up to Hadi.

"Did you see how I made him go?" he asked.

"Yes, sir."

"Your turn." Master Aziz was looking at Hadi. He told the camel to sit and slowly the animal bent down on his knees and slumped his bottom to the ground. He let out a low moan as if all this getting up and down was painful.

Master Aziz helped Hadi get onto the camel. He felt awkward with the big hump.

"Do I sit here?" asked Hadi pointing behind the hump. Hadi heard laughter ringing around him.

"Sit in the saddle, boy." Master Aziz slapped the saddle to show Hadi where to sit. Hadi scrunched his bottom until he felt he was securely in the saddle. Master Aziz tapped the camel's sides with the whip and told the camel to get up. It did and wobbled as it stood. This caused Hadi to lose his balance and fall off the side.

"The idea is to ride the camel!" shouted one boy.

"Get up, get up! You can't let the camel know you are afraid!" shouted Master Aziz.

"He's like a fat fly stuck on its back!" shouted one of the boys.

"No he looks like a fish," said the smaller boy.

Master Aziz's face tightened. He turned to the two boys. "Rashim, Faisal. Go back to the house! You do not belong here!" The boys jumped from the stands and ran towards the big house. Were they his master's sons? Hadi had only seen them at the bleachers the day before.

He hated to be embarrassed. He wiped the sand and dust from his shirt and walked around the camel next to Master Aziz. He stood shaking his head. The camel got back down on the ground and Hadi climbed aboard again. Hadi ignored the teasing going on behind him. This time he landed firmly in the saddle. He held the reins tightly, jerking the camel backwards. The camel swaggered from side to side. Master Aziz grabbed the reins and walked them past the track to the open desert.

Heat waves danced all around them for as far as the eye could see. Everything looked like it was quivering. Patches of brown, dead, grass lay here and there where hungry camels had eaten the desert clean. There was nothing but the sun, the dry earth, Master Aziz, the camel and Hadi.

"We'll take it slow, okay?" asked Master Aziz. "You must learn to hold on with your legs. Squeeze them tight."

Hadi squeezed as hard as he could. He didn't want to fall off again.

Master Aziz showed Hadi how to make the camel turn left and right and go backwards. He showed him how to make the camel obey his commands. It wasn't always easy since the camel often wanted to do things his own way. Over and over they practiced. The sun rose in the sky and beat down on them. Finally, day one of training was over.

When it was time to go home, Hadi climbed off the camel. His legs felt weak and wobbly and he found it difficult to walk. That night his legs ached and throbbed. "I have to do this every day?" he moaned to himself. He rubbed his legs and to ease the pain and tossed and turned for hours. If it wasn't the pain that kept him awake, it was memories of Asim. Sometime that night, Hadi fell asleep. The new day came quickly.

Each day after breakfast and chores, before the sun reached its highest and hottest point in the sky, Master Aziz and Hadi walked out to the desert. Hadi's legs got used to riding and soon the pain was gone. He felt natural on the camel. Even the boys who taunted him earlier lost their eagerness to tease Hadi. He had learned well and was on his way to becoming a real camel jockey.

Hadi heard the other boys talk about him at breakfast. "Master Aziz is going to let him race first," said one.

"He's going to win all the races," said another.

They're jealous, thought Hadi. Then he thought about the young Sri Lanka boy who was in the local papers. The boy, who was only seven, was killed by the other young boys at another souk. He was a good camel jockey. He had won several races and the other boys were so jealous that they decided it would be better if he wasn't around. So, they killed him. It was that simple, yet horrifying to Hadi. He decided it was a risk he had to take if he ever wanted to return home.

~   ~   ~

For a month, Hadi learned the basics of riding a camel. It was early September and there was only one more week until the racing season started. As Master Aziz and Hadi walked to the track, Master Aziz made an announcement. "Today you learn to race!"

Hadi's pace quickened at this news. He was scared too. *What if I fall off? What if I get killed?* Instead of going out to the desert, Master Aziz stopped at the track.

The camel bent down and Hadi climbed on its back. This time Master Aziz tied a rope around Hadi's waist. The rope was attached to the saddle.

"So you don't fall off," said Master Aziz. "Camels can run very fast. With the wind pushing against you, you could fall off." Hadi wasn't sure if he should be thankful to be tied onto a camel's back or scared to death. He pulled the rope to make sure it was secure. "What if the camel trips and falls?" he asked.

Master Aziz paused for a second. "It won't."

The camel stood up. Hadi guided him onto the track. Master Aziz stood on the side and leaned against the rickety old fence. Hadi looked back. "Remember what I told you!" shouted Master Aziz.

Hadi swallowed what little spit was in his mouth. He took a deep breath and let out a scream that would have scared vultures away. The camel took off as if it were afraid something was chasing it. It did not like his high, shrill voice. Hadi had a hard time slowing him down.

"A-yee!" shouted Hadi. His voice was so high it reminded him of the screech his little sister Samra made when she was caught during a game of hide and seek or touch wood.

Hadi steered the camel around the track. The wind blew in his face and he squinted hard to keep the sand, wind and sun from blinding him. His head started to hurt and he felt like his brain was crashing against his skull. The ride was the bumpiest ride he had ever had. Hadi didn't want to go on. He felt like he was going to fall off.

His legs became weak and gripping the camel took all of his energy. Hadi saw Master Aziz jumping with his arms in the air.

Hadi cracked the whip on the camel's rump and shouted high and loud. The camel bolted ahead at full speed, legs flailing out in front, ears pinned to his head. The quickness caught Hadi's breath and he felt like passing out. Now he was coming in to homestretch. It was time to give it all he and the camel had. He screamed again loudly, "A-yee!" The camel's body thrust forward trying to escape Hadi's yell. Hadi hit the camel on its rump and shouted until they crossed the finish line.

Hadi pulled back on the reins and stopped his yelling. The camel, thankfully, came to a stop in front of Master Aziz, snorted a few times and shook his head.

"You got it, Hadi! You can make that camel run!" Master Aziz smiled at him and stroked the camel. Hadi and the camel breathed heavily, both catching their breath.

Hadi sat in a daze the same way Asim had. His head throbbed and his entire body shook. Sweat dripped off his face like a leaky faucet and the hot sun made matters worse. He felt sick to his stomach; the world was spinning and then darkness.

Chapter 8

Recovery

Hadi awoke in his bed. It was dark except for a small light in the corner of the room. He looked around trying to find someone. He saw
no one. His head throbbed and his legs ached like he had broken
them. He was naked too. *How did I get here?* he thought. *The last
thing I remember was sitting on the camel.* Hadi remembered the
day's events in his head and went over them again and again. Then
he remembered feeling ill and passing out. "Oh no," he moaned.
He lay staring at the ceiling. "What are they going to do to me?"
Tears started falling down his dirty cheek. *I've disappointed Master
Aziz.* Hadi was sure he would be sent away or worse, killed.

"I'm no good," he whispered. "Mama! I'm sorry, Mama." Hadi
pulled the blanket to his eyes and wiped them. He felt a hand on his
forehead.

"Hadi," said a quiet voice.

Hadi quickly looked up. No one was there. He scanned the room,
and still it was dark and empty with only a glimmer of light coming
from Master Aziz's house.

"Who's there?" he asked his voice trembling. He could hardly get
the words out. His lips felt tight and jagged as they had been
chapped and dry from the sun.

Silence.

Hadi scurried underneath his blankets again and closed his eyes. If only his headache would go away. It felt like a fist was pounding him in the side of the head over and over. He covered his head with his arms and squeezed tight. "Stop hurting," he cried.

"You will be fine," said the voice.

Hadi sat up. "Mama?" He looked around. "Is that you?"

Silence.

Distant laughter echoed through the souk. It was the boys and men finishing their dinner.

Hadi sat with his back against the wall and watched his room carefully. He tried to make out where the door was. A stream of light flickered under the blanket that blocked the doorway. There was so little light he couldn't see shadows. He rubbed his temples and coughed. Sand mixed with blood landed on the edge of his mattress. Hadi swiped his hand through it by accident. "Ah, gross." Hadi wrapped his blanket around his waist, got up and stumbled to the doorway. His legs hurt and felt as if they were about to buckle under him. He pushed the blanket covering the door aside and stepped into the cool night air. Hadi breathed in and out deeply. He heard laughter coming from the big house and knew that everyone must be there eating dinner. Hadi limped to the water trough in the camel's corral. He splashed the water on his head and in his mouth. Kneeling on the ground, he heard the voice again.

"You will race, you will go home. Do not worry, Hadi."

These words comforted him. He looked up into the sky. Only the stars twinkled down at him. "Don't go. Please stay with me. I'm so scared." Hadi slumped against the trough. Was the voice in his head? Hadi wondered. It was so clear. A roar of laughter echoed throughout the yard as if they were laughing at Hadi. The laughter rolled over him like a wave and Hadi felt sick.

"I am always with you, Hadi. Always."

A breeze swept through gathering some dust. Hadi looked up to the stars and felt the blood pulsating through the veins in his head. Then something moved under the olive tree.

"Asim?" Hadi grabbed the side of the trough and pulled himself up. He took a few steps towards the figure and rubbed his eyes. There was nothing but the tree. He scanned the sky, black and cloudless so every star twinkled brightly. A shooting star fell brilliantly through the atmosphere. "Asim, is that you?" Hadi shouted. "Where are you?" Hadi sat at the base of the olive tree, the same place he and Asim had spent many nights talking. He missed his only friend at the souk and wished they were together again. Hadi wished for many things. He rested his head back on the tree and watched the stars above. His stomach growled. It had occurred to him that no one brought him food or water. They put him on his mattress to suffer alone. "If I were home, Mama would take good care of me," he said. Grabbing his stomach so empty and full of hunger pains he noticed one star in particular. It blinked brightly as if it were sending an SOS. Hadi imagined it was the same star shining brightly over his home in Pakistan. *Maybe it's Mama sending me a message*, he thought and smiled.

"Thank you," he whispered. He wasn't sure to whom. Maybe someone somewhere would hear him. Hadi walked back into his room. He dressed in a clean shirt and crawled back to bed.

As he lay there, a figure appeared in the door.

"Hadi," said Master Aziz. "Are you feeling better?"

Hadi sat up. "Yes, I think so."

"Good. In one week you'll be racing!" Master Aziz walked over and grabbed his shoulders. "You will win, right?"

"I hope so," Hadi wriggled his shoulders from Master Aziz's grip. Master Aziz growled and said, "I know so. Get some sleep, Hadi. You'll need your rest!"

Hadi lay back down. Still no one brought him anything to eat. No one really cared about Hadi and he knew this. The boys soon gathered in the room talking about the races. There was no lantern or candle to light the room so all lay down on their mattresses and giggled and talked for a few minutes more. Then, the room was silent. The night was quiet.

Hadi tossed and turned he was sure for hours. His stomach gurgled loudly. He heard some boys next to him snicker. "Go to sleep, Hadi. You're keeping us up!"

"Make that stomach of yours shut up!"

Hadi ignored their comments as he always had. He rolled over and faced the cold dirt wall. A camel groaned in the night. Somehow, sometime that night, Hadi fell asleep.

He had wonderful dreams of winning camel races and people cheering his name.

"Hadi, Hadi!" they shouted.

Then his dream turned to a nightmare as Hadi saw his mother crying over a pile of dirt, Hadi's grave.

"Hadi, Hadi!" she moaned.

Hadi woke up suddenly to the morning.

Chapter 9

The Great Camel Race

The week passed uneventfully. Hadi did his chores every day and then practiced with Master Aziz. He began to feel confident on top of the camel and learned to become almost one with the animal. His body moved with the camel's as it sped down the racetrack. He was given goggles to wear to keep flying pieces of dirt and sand out of his face. Hadi was beginning to feel like a real camel jockey!

The night before the big races, Hadi had a hard time getting to sleep. He rubbed his eyes and looked about the room. Morning had come faster than he wished. "Just one more hour of sleep," he whispered and yawned. Something lay at the end of his mattress. He scrambled to it and unfolded a green shirt and a pair of blue jeans.

"What are these for?" he asked.

One of the boys, Nabil in his room spoke up. He leaned up against the wall and looked at Hadi. "Master Aziz got them for you. He gives his favorite jockeys new clothes to race in. You must be a favorite, Hadi." The other boys snickered and whispered. Some shook their heads and ignored Hadi. Not all the boys would be going to the races. There were still chores to do at the souk.

Hadi didn't know what to think. He felt badly because the other boys were still wearing the long white shirts. He quickly dressed. Underneath his mattress laid his secret treasure. *I won't race without it!* He quickly grabbed his rock. It was small enough that he could easily hide it inside a pocket in his new pants. He sat on the edge of his mattress and watched the sun slowly rise and peek through his window.

"Today is the big race, Hadi. Are you ready?" asked Nabil.

"Yes." Hadi didn't want to talk to anyone about the races. He always was teased. *Not today*, thought Hadi. *You are not ruining my day!*

"Don't get your hopes up. There will be other jockeys there, better and smarter than you." Nabil stuck his feet out from the blanket eyeing Hadi.

Hadi said nothing as he buttoned his shirt and raced to eat breakfast. Behind him, he heard Nabil laughing.

After breakfast, Hadi meandered to the driveway. Older boys were loading the camels onto trailers while Master Aziz shouted at them. "Get a move on! Show them who's boss! What are you stupid?" he shouted, cracking the whip not so much at the camels, but at the boys. The camels were loaded one by one onto the trailer.

"Can I help?" asked Hadi.

Master Aziz snarled. "Just stay out of our way. Your job comes later." He cracked a whip on one camel's rump and a young boy, not much older than Hadi pulled him into the trailer. The camels fought every minute. They groaned and yanked back on the rope so the boy was lifted into the air. Master Aziz cracked the whip on their rumps again and again.

Dust blew in plumes across the dirt road and the camels snorted and bolted their heads every time they were pulled or whipped. Finally, the last one was loaded onto the fifth trailer. Master Aziz was racing twenty different camels this week. A pick-up truck stopped abruptly beside Hadi. "Get in," hollered the driver. Hadi climbed up the back and fell among fifteen or so other young boys.

He knew all of them, but hardly ever spoke to any. Some were there to help keep the camels clean but only Hadi and three other boys were there to race. Hadi scanned the faces. *Good, Nabil isn't here*, he thought. They all looked at Hadi, some grinning, and some staring blankly. Hadi hung his head and looked at his sandals. They were well worn and torn in some places. His overgrown toenails were caked with dirt and between his toes, sand stuck like glue. He tried to rub some off so he wouldn't have to look or talk to the boys. It felt like sandpaper and he rubbed until his skin turned red.

The pick-up truck raced behind the trailers. The vehicles flew down the long stretch of gray road. Hadi held on to the side of the truck and felt the wind in his hair. It was different than riding a camel in the desert. The wind made by the truck was stronger and Hadi felt as though his hair might come right out of his scalp. The truck sped along. Hadi looked to his right and saw the huge fence running alongside the road. In the distance, he saw small shacks and an occasional camel grazing on isolated shrubs and grasses. The sky was so pale it hardly looked blue and heat waves wiggled on the horizon. Some of the boys talked, most stared at each other with a blankness and sadness Hadi understood.

Suddenly, the boy next to Hadi nudged him. "You ever been to Dubai?" he asked.

"No," said Hadi. "Is that where we're going?"

"Don't you know where we're going?" the boy asked, shaking his head.

"No one told me. I was told I was going to race." Hadi looked at his hands.

They were brown and callused. He rubbed them together to give him something to do.

"Dubai has the biggest races around," said the boy. "It's going to be crowded there today."

Hadi said nothing. He looked at the road behind him and wished he was home. An hour later, the trailers and trucks finally pulled into a large parking lot. They stopped and all the boys piled out. Hadi looked around. Young boys sat, walked and played in the middle of the parking lot. The trainers and older boys unloaded the camels and divvied out the grain and water. Hadi followed the others to the shady side of the truck, sat down on the dirt and waited.

Master Aziz showed up about half an hour later. He had a clipboard and rambled off names. Hadi listened as he heard his name called. "Hadi, you will ride King in the third race," said Master Aziz, who continued down his list without pausing for a breath. When he was finished, he spoke to Hadi again.

"Follow those boys. They'll tell you where to go."

Hadi nodded and scurried after the other three camel jockeys. He followed them to the corral. Camels ate grain and sipped water, and then one by one each camel threw up. "That's disgusting," said one of the boys. Master Aziz came up behind them, laughing.

Hadi scrunched his nose and found the camel named King. He was huge! Much bigger than the young camels Hadi rode at the souk. An older boy approached him. "You Hadi?" he asked.

"Yes."

"This is King. He's strong and fast. You've been weighed yet?"

"No," said Hadi.

The boy took Hadi back to the truck and pulled out a scale. "Step on it," said the boy. Hadi did and watched the little red arrow bounce back and forth. "Forty five kilos! Let's say it was forty, okay?"

Hadi nodded.

They started to walk back to the corral. "How old are you?" asked the boy.

"Nine," said Hadi.

"Too bad. This will probably be your last race. You weigh too much." The boy crawled between the wires of the fence and saddled King.

"I've never raced before. I can't be done already." Hadi hung his head and wiggled his toes. He felt like he was getting nowhere fast.

"Let's see how you do today. Have a helmet?"

Hadi shook his head no. The young boy scurried to a trunk and pulled out a red and black bike helmet. He strapped it on. In the distance, Hadi could hear the crowd cheering as the first race was under way.

Another half hour went by. Hadi was hot. The other boys climbed on their camels and headed towards the grandstands. They looked tired to Hadi. Most never even smiled. They had that lost look to their faces. Jockeys and boys from other souks sat in groups or chased each other around. Some of them looked so small. Smaller than Hadi, which meant they had to be younger.

"Hadi," he heard his name over the boy's laughter and the cheering crowd. He quickly ran to the corral. "You're up next," said the boy who had helped him earlier. He made the camel get down on his knees. Hadi climbed up behind the hump. He planted his bottom on top of the bristly fabric. When he tried to sit up, he couldn't. He was firmly attached. The jeans he had on had sticky stuff, some kind of material attached to them. Hadi pulled himself up harder the second time and listened to the crunching sounds of the material as his bottom separated from the saddle. He giggled. "What's this stuff for on my seat?" he asked.

"It's to hold you on the camel," said Master Aziz, who just appeared from behind the camel. "I can't tie you on like at the souk."

"So if I fall I off, I will just fall instead of hang?" asked Hadi.

Master Aziz nodded. "It's safer for the camel."

Safer for me too, thought Hadi.

Hadi made a clicking sound with his mouth and the camel rose, high. He was above the truck and everyone else. His heart raced with excitement. It was Hadi's first race! The heat, the smell and his nerves all brewed together in a way that made Hadi eager to get the race over. Hadi looked down at the boy and smiled. The boy held onto the reins and led the camel with Hadi on its back to the grandstand entrance.

They were one of the first camels there and Hadi got a clear look at the grandstand. He saw the rich sitting in the middle, the best

seats in the place. Then those with less sat on special places desig-
nated for them and on the outskirts sat pale-faced tourists with
cameras and binoculars.

An announcer shouted through a loudspeaker in Arabic. The
third race was about to begin. Then he spoke in English for the tourists' benefit. Hadi gently kicked King and persuaded him onto the
racetrack. Many others followed. All the camels had colorful ribbons
draped from their saddles and necks. King had the most beautiful
ribbons Hadi had ever seen. They flowed over his neck and rump in
rivers of red, black and gold. They danced in the wind and
reminded Hadi of the kites he flew back home.

People stood in the stands cheering the jockeys and camels on
to victory. The young jockeys lined their camels up behind a white
line painted in the sand and anxiously waited for the race to start.
Hadi looked about him frantically trying not to get in the way of the
other camels. All the riders were boys, most younger than he. They
were lighter too and had a better chance of winning. Hadi grinded
his teeth and kept King as calm as he could. The other jockeys
kicked their camels and hollered at each other. It all became a blur
to Hadi. He didn't want to be there.

The roar of the crowd, the heat, the confusion was enough to
make his head spin. He pulled in the reins tightly and his elbow
pushed against the small object he had hidden in his pant's pocket.
"I will do this," he said. "I will win!"

Hadi didn't hear the signal to go. King did and jolted forward.
King's raced before, thought Hadi, relieved that one of them knew
what to do. He stuck like glue to the camel's hump and grabbed on
with his legs. Feeling more comfortable he crouched over and took
the racing position.

King ran with the power of many camels. There were several
camels behind the leader. Hadi looked back. All he saw was a ball
of dust behind him growing as big as a cloud. He heard the rumble
of heavy padded feet and knew the other camels were close

behind. He had to focus on the ones in front of him. *How can I get past them*? he wondered. Around the track they ran, finishing the first half mile. Hadi still was unable to get King to go any faster.

"I must get home!" he shouted. "Move, dumb camel, move!" Nothing seemed to work. Flashes of his mother, then his little sister popped into his mind. He remembered her shrilly voice.

"A-yee!" shouted Hadi.

King flattened his ears back on his head. He took off like a bullet as Hadi kept yelling, "A-yee!"

They passed one camel, then another until there were only two camels in front of them. King ran at a full loping gallop. Hadi could barely see the finish line ahead. Balls of dust blew in his face and he swallowed sand and dirt. He tried to yell. Nothing would come out. Hadi opened his mouth wide and pushed with all his might, so that a sound might leap out, but still nothing. Instead, Hadi choked and coughed on the dirt spewing in his face.

Suddenly, the camel, just ten feet in front of King tripped. Hadi watched in horror as the camel went down. He looked behind him to see a mob of camels rushing their way. When he looked forward at the camel now down on the ground, the young jockey disappeared under the camel's heavy body. Hadi and King passed them. As they did, Hadi saw the boy underneath struggling to get off the camel, but nothing he did set him free. The camel tried to stand up. Back down he fell with a thud! Hadi heard a loud scream and looked back only to see the mob of camels trample the fallen camel and the young boy. It happened so fast. The camel was there in front of him one minute and gone the next.

"AHHH!" screamed Hadi again and again. He closed his eyes tight and crouched low. He did not know King had passed the leader and was racing across the finish line. King knew it was over before Hadi and slowly came to a stop. Hadi's body trembled and he stayed hunched over the camel grasping the brown hair in his fists. The crowd stood on their feet and cheered "Hadi, Hadi, Hadi!" He didn't hear the cheers.

"Bang!" A loud gunshot echoed through the racetrack and the grandstands. Hadi jumped in his seat at the sound. There was a moment of silence as the crowd turned heads to see what happened. As quickly as they stopped, the chants started again. What he heard was the gunshot that killed the injured camel. The sound rang through his body and made every hair stand on end. An ambulance drove in front of Hadi and King, its sirens blaring. *Was the boy dead? Or maybe messed up,* he thought. Either way, he had no life. He tried to look to see the boy, but camels and people got in his way.

Master Aziz raced out and grabbed King. He led them to the winner's circle and pulled Hadi off the saddle. The stranger who had earlier bought some camels from Master Aziz rushed over.

"Sheik Syed, King won!" shouted Master Aziz. The sheik kissed Master Aziz on the nose and he received more kisses from the crowd gathering around. Someone brought a bucket of water for King. Master Aziz patted him on the head and kissed King. Hadi was pushed aside by the crowd and shuffled to the back. He rubbed his sore bottom and slowly walked back to the truck. The ambulance sped off towards the hospital. Hadi sat in the pick up truck waiting for Master Aziz.

He slouched down against the hot metal, exhausted from the race. Lifting the lid to the cooler, he fished around for something cool to drink. The ice had melted and the bottles of water floated in tepid water. Hadi pulled out a bottle and wiped it along his forehead. He coughed up sand and spit it over the side of the truck.

He opened the bottle and took a drink. The cold, wet liquid oozed down his throat, yet as nice as it felt, it made him cough even more. He felt it go down to the pit of his stomach. Little glory was given to him but he didn't care. He closed his eyes and dreamed about getting home.

An hour later, Master Aziz appeared at the truck counting the money he had earned that day.

"Today was a good day-eh, Hadi?" he grinned.

Hadi nodded, too weak to say anything.

"Tomorrow you race again. You race until the week is over," said Master Aziz.

"Go eat, Hadi. You need your strength." Master Aziz pointed to a small kiosk where rice and noodles were cooking. Hadi lumbered over and got his dinner. When he returned, some of the boys were pitching tents.

"This one is yours," shouted a young boy. "The winner gets to sleep in here." He pointed to the opening and beckoned Hadi to come over. Too tired to argue and too weak to care, Hadi did as he was told and collapsed inside the tent.

Chapter 10
Hadi's Plan

Hadi rose early the next morning. His legs ached so badly he could hardly move them. He sat up and tried to stretch them, wiggling his toes first then tightening and resting his muscles. He wiped the sleep from his eyes and heard someone shouting his name outside.

"Hadi! Hadi!"

Slowly he crept to the opening in the tent and peered out. The sun hit his face like a hot cloth. He squinted and focused on the man calling him. "Oh no," Hadi moaned. It was Master Aziz doing the roll call for the morning races. Hadi backed into the tent and buried his head in his hands. Tired and weak, he wanted nothing more to do with races or camels. *I could just lie here and pretend I'm dead.* Hadi lay very still.

He lay on his back and closed his eyes tight. Suddenly a vision came to him. He saw his mother fetching the water, preparing breakfast, cleaning the clothes, and whacking the blankets clean of bugs and dirt. She never complained, never whined or moaned. Hadi heard his brothers and sister laughing and splashing water at him as they played in the nearby stream. He pictured the rows of rice in the paddy, the lush green paddies, his father at one end, friends at the other, all working together. *Life is so different now,* he thought.

Hadi put his arm over his eyes to try to block out the headache he felt coming on. Suddenly, something grabbed his feet and the earth moved under him. Rocks and sand scratched his back as he was dragged out from the tent. The sun glared in his eyes and he quickly covered them. Laughter rang all around. Hadi lay on the ground surrounded by a group of boys, he knew from the souk. All were laughing and pointing.

"Hadi. It's roll call. Get up!" said Darim.

Hadi quickly stood up and looked at the boys. They hadn't dragged him far. He wiped his pants and pulled his shirt down. Master Aziz was by the pick up truck, watching and smiling. Then he waved for Hadi to come to him. Hadi nodded, ignored the taunts behind him and walked over to Master Aziz.

"Good morning, Hadi. Did you sleep well?" Master Aziz talked and wrote at the same time, never looking up at Hadi.

"Yes, sir."

"Good. Because you will be racing three times today." Master Aziz chuckled. "You will make some good money this week, Hadi. As long as you don't get killed."

Hadi faintly smiled and nodded his head. The sun felt hotter than usual and he wiped his brow with his shirtsleeve. It was already stained well from the day before. A long, grungy smear stained his green riding shirt leaving behind a dark streak.

"I will keep your money until the races are over. When we get back to the souk, I will give it to you then. Too many greedy little urchins around and you have no place to keep it safe here."

Again, Hadi nodded. This sounded like a good idea, as long as Master Aziz kept his end of the deal and paid Hadi fairly. Master Aziz gave Hadi the times of the races. One thing was certain, there was no time to waste.

Hadi raced the three races and won the second race. For five days, he raced and each day he won at least one race. Soon

Hadi's name was spreading around the racetrack. He was becoming famous.

Hadi had a plan. When he wasn't racing, he was thinking and when he wasn't thinking he was sleeping. Even in his dreams, his plan would unfold. He knew it wouldn't be easy escaping the souk. How would he leave unnoticed? Which way would he go?

One day in between races, Hadi decided that once they were back at the souk and he had his money in his hand he would make a run for it. Everyone would be tired and Master Aziz promised the boys who raced a few days off.

Hadi sat at the base of the truck's wheel in the shade and closed his eyes. He pictured in his mind, Master Aziz handing him the money he had won from the races. Hadi would be gracious and thank his master. He would act the same as always; go to dinner with everyone, and get ready for bed. Once they were all lying down for the night, Hadi would tell the boys that he had to go to the bathroom, after all a trip to the hole in the ground wasn't unusual. Then, in the dark of the night, he would run through the hole in the fence and out to the road.

Hadi kicked some dirt and watched it plow up into his sandal. *Do I go to Abu Dhabi, where they will expect me to go? Or do I go in the other direction?* Hadi wasn't sure because he didn't know where the road led in the other direction. Everyone would assume he would go to the city. "I will go the other way," he said and smiled.

"Hadi! You're up!" shouted Master Aziz as he rounded the corner of the truck. "Get up, boy! It's your turn to race!"

Hadi quickly jumped up and smiled at Master Aziz. "Yes, sir," he said and ran to his camel. He felt Master Aziz watching him and probably wondering why Hadi was so cheerful.

Hadi was confident about his plan. It changed his mood and his entire outlook on life. He was going home and no one would stop him! And it would all happen in just a matter of days!

On the sixth day, the camels were loaded and the boys climbed back into the pick-up truck for the ride home. Hadi was glad to be done with the races. Only the one boy was hurt the entire time and for this, the camel owners were happy. If word got out in the newspapers that a boy was hurt or killed, the owners would be very angry. It was grueling and tiring and every bone and muscle ached in Hadi's body. Large, round calluses marred the palms of his hands. He actually looked forward to sleeping on his own mattress despite its putrid smells and bloody stains.

Some time passed before Hadi recognized where he was. Back through the busy city of Abu Dhabi and its lush greenery, the road that led to the camel souk was welcoming. Hadi figured this would be the last time he saw Abu Dhabi. Part of his plan was to find the next city in the opposite direction and hopefully find someone to take him to the nearest port. He didn't have enough money to take an airplane home. Maybe he could catch a boat and leave the same way he came!

The trucks and trailers soon pulled into the souk. Hadi was out of the truck before it even came to a complete stop. He rushed to his room and fell on his mattress. That night he slept soundly.

~   ~   ~

The next day Master Aziz handed out the earnings to the boys. "You did well, Hadi," he said. "I have big plans for you." He handed Hadi a wad of dirhams.

"Thank you," said Hadi and he quickly rushed back to his room. He lifted the corner of his mattress to reveal his old pair of pants. Looking around to make sure no one was in the room, he stuffed the wad into a pocket with what little money he had already earned. *Will it be enough?* he wondered. It would have to be. He said the name Karachi over and over in his mind because that was the port he needed to get to. He prayed every night to God and asked that his planned escape would go well. He would have to trust strangers to get him home. There was no other way. He hoped he would have enough money to pay them and as long as he got home, he didn't care what it would take.

The few days felt like years to Hadi. The days were cooler as the winter season approached. Nothing changed in the souk. Hadi worked like always, doing the same things he had always done. He didn't even ride the camels but was told to keep their pens clean and the animals fed. Hadi noticed Master Aziz paying more attention to the newer, younger boys that had recently arrived. Word was spreading around the souk. With the new arrivals, some of the older boys would be let go. Still, it couldn't be soon enough for Hadi. Every night he imagined sitting down for dinner with his family. He thought about sleeping with his brothers and sister and how warm he would be.

His escape and return home kept him going. He knew that if he stayed, his chances of racing next year were slim. It was over. His days in the camel souk were limited one way or another!

Chapter 11

The Escape

Hadi's plan was already faltered. He had decided to make his escape just a few days after they got back. Each time he thought he had a chance, something happened. One night as he was making his way out the door to go to the "bathroom", Master Aziz caught him and sent him back to the room. Another night, Hadi tripped over a bucket and made so much noise that it caused two guards to run out into the yard and find him. He had fallen on the ground. A third time, Hadi almost made it to the fence when another boy going to the bathroom saw him. He yelled at Hadi, "Where are you going?"

Hadi, pretending to be walking in his sleep mumbled something and walked right back to his room. It was hopeless. Every effort failed and Hadi was feeling discouraged. A month had already passed and Hadi was lined up with the other boys to receive their monthly pay. Master Aziz stood waiting with a clip board and a small pile of bills. He called out each boys name and one by one they received their pay. When he got to Hadi, he put his hands on Hadi's shoulders and smiled, laughing a little. Hadi looked into his dark brown eyes. He had never really looked at Master Aziz before. The other boys sneered at Hadi. He was still a favorite to Master Aziz.

Hadi held out his hand and graciously accepted the pay. "Thank you, sir," he said and tightly held the small coins in the palm of his hand. Then he rushed back to his room. He pulled back the mattress and retrieved his pants. Bills and coins fell out of the pockets. Quickly, Hadi stuffed them back in.

"So that's where you keep your earnings," came a voice from the corner of the room. Hadi spun around and saw Saad, one of the older boys who constantly made fun of him, leaning against the wall, arms crossed in front of him, grinning. "Hadi, you should not keep your money from your family. That has to be sent back home."

"Sent home?" said Hadi. He rolled the pants in his arms and quickly sat on top of his mattress. "I should be sent back home."

"Give it to me, boy," said Saad. He walked slowly towards Hadi. "I will make sure it goes to your poor parents."

Hadi felt his heart flip inside his chest. He had to do something to protect his money. He had planned to escape, maybe tonight would be the night. He would try anyway. He needed all the money he had.

"Give it here." Saad reached out his hand. Hadi refused to budge. He held on even tighter to the pants and stood up.

"Leave me alone!" he screamed. "Just leave me alone!"

The door was wide open. Saad rushed him. Faster than a lizard, Hadi scooted between the mattresses and Saad. Saad grabbed his shirt and pulled him back. Hadi fell but slipped right out of his shirt so all he had on was his undershirt. He stood and raced out the door.

"Hadi. Get back here!" shouted Saad.

Boys in the yard stopped their work and watched as Hadi ran. Saad was not chasing him though, just calling his name loudly. Hadi ran toward the big building where Master Aziz lived. He remembered where the hole was and looked back one last time to see what everyone was doing. They had gone back to their work. No one was paying attention to Hadi, at least as far as he could tell. *Maybe they think I'm going to the master's house*, he thought. *Or maybe Saad just thinks I'm hiding my pants.* For the first time in a long time, Hadi smiled. His journey home was about to begin but he hadn't planned for it to occur in broad daylight! This was his chance. Everyone was busy or working and Hadi could slip out.

Hadi found the hole and squeezed through it. He stood up and looked around. In the distance, he saw clouds. "That's the way to Abu Dhabi," he said. He looked down the road in the opposite direction. "I was going to go that way," he said looking away from the familiar city. "Now what I am going to do?"

Clouds puffed and billowed over the city like big bullies; always threatening to rain yet rarely pouring down. The white puffy clouds lingering over the shoreline beckoned to Hadi and he knew there was a port just a few miles in front of him. Yet, he wanted to run to the unknown, in the direction they would least expect him to go. His gut told him to head for Abu Dhabi. Just then, he heard someone back in the souk ask, "Where is Hadi? He has work to do!"

Panicked, Hadi tightly held his bundle of pants with the money and ran as fast as he could down the road. The dull black pavement, nearly white now from the sun was hot as a griddle. Hadi took a few more steps and slowed to a walk. He could still see the souk behind him and knew he hadn't gone very far. "What am I nuts?" he asked aloud. No water, no food, no shirt and a blazing hot sun beating down on him was suicide. Hadi focused on the clouds ahead and kept walking.

There was no sign of life anywhere. Hadi walked on the pavement in the direction of the clouds. He kept looking back at the souk to see if anyone was following. No one did. Maybe Saad had forgotten about Hadi now. Hadi's confidence rose and he walked swinging one arm back and forth while the other arm held the wadded pants in place. He also found it was cooler to do this. The sun shined down on his bare arms. His mouth and throat were soon dry and even licking his lips didn't help. He kept walking and pictured the river near his hometown. *Cool water, smooth and flowing...like this road...smooth and flowing toward the city...I will be home soon!* There, he would have all the water he could wish for.

Behind him, Hadi heard a car approaching. Dread filled his body. They were coming to get him! He quickly looked around. There was no where to hide! The road and the land were flat and not one bush or tree was found anywhere. Hadi stuck out boldly against the arid brown backdrop. He watched as the car raced by, stopped and backed up nearly hitting him. Hadi's heart sunk. He had been caught.

He watched as a man cranked down a window. It wasn't anyone he recognized. "Boy, why aren't you at the souk?" asked the man.

Hadi's heart pounded and sadness draped over his body. *Now I'm doomed. This man will send me back*, thought Hadi. He paused trying to think of something to say, something that would sound reasonable. After all, a young foreigner walking the street by himself could only mean he was running away.

Well, sir," began Hadi. "Master Aziz sent me on an errand to the city. You see I am the greatest camel jockey the souk has ever had. I am like a son to Master Aziz." Hadi held his head up proudly and continued to walk. The car rolled slowly beside him. The man inside looked Hadi from head to toe.

"Can you prove that you mean so much to Master Aziz?"

Hadi beamed and quickly pulled out his pants. He dug in the pockets and showed the man his stash of money. He shook the pants so the man could hear some of the coins rattle inside. "Master Aziz gave this to me to buy some things," said Hadi.

"Well, if you are like a son to Master Aziz, perhaps your master wouldn't mind if a friendly stranger drove his boy to town, rather than letting him walk in this heat."

"Maybe," said Hadi. "How do I know I can trust you?"

"I guess you can't know. You'll have to trust your gut. By the way, where is your shirt?"

Hadi shrugged and looked at the sky. It's hot out here! I rolled them up with my pants."

The man eyed Hadi. He looked back in the direction of the souk and then forward to the city. "Never mind. Get in and I'll take you to the town." The car stopped and Hadi jumped in the back seat.

"Thank you, sir." The car sped up and raced down the road. Hadi took one last look behind him. The camel souk grew smaller and smaller until Hadi could no longer see it. He scratched his head, smiled a little and thought about home and his family waiting for him.

He faced forward staring out the front window. "It won't be easy," he whispered. He held on tight to his money and looked at all the camel crossing signs they passed until they reached Abu Dhabi.

Chapter 12

Homeward Bound

"Here we are," said the man. He pulled his car into a parking spot in downtown Abu Dhabi. Hadi looked around. The last time he was here, he went through the city so fast he didn't have time to really check it out. He climbed out of the car.

"Thank you, sir."

"Do you know where you are going?" asked the man.

Hadi looked around. He had no idea. He couldn't tell that to the man. "I sure do," he said. "Thank you, again." Hadi turned and walked down a street. He noticed on the side, between some buildings there were kiosks filled with things to buy. Hadi headed straight for them. When he looked back, the man who had driven him was gone.

Hadi kept walking. People crowded around the kiosks haggling over prices. He saw watches and perfume, gold jewelry, and clothing. He thought about his little sister and mother. *I will get them something pretty.* As he waded past kiosks filled with finery it occurred to him that he needed the money to get home. That was his goal and fine gifts would have to come another day.

He wanted to get his mother something special. He felt his eyes swell with tears and turned to walk away. As he turned he bumped into something. That something bent down and stared into Hadi's eyes. Hadi looked up and saw a pale faced woman looking intently back at him. She was unlike any of the women he saw. The other women here covered their faces with dark veils. This one showed her face. Her skin was fair and her hair was light brown and wavy. She was much lighter skinned than Hadi. *She's not from these parts,* thought Hadi.

She smiled. "What's wrong?" she asked.

Hadi felt heat rise to his face. He couldn't take his eyes of her.

"Are you a movie star?" he asked.

"No. A tourist. Now tell me what is wrong." She knelt down in front him, her knees touching the ground. A man, who was standing behind the tourist, as fair skinned and light haired as she, turned and smiled at Hadi too.

"I wanted to buy my mother some perfume and I don't have enough money." Hadi looked to the ground and scuffed his feet.

"Where is your mother?" asked the woman.

"She lives in Pakistan."

"That's far away. Where is your father?"

"He's there too. That's where I'm from and I am trying to get back home tonight."

"By yourself?"

"Yes."

"Why are you in Abu Dhabi?" asked the man.

Hadi didn't know what to tell them. Should he be truthful or lie like he had been all along. He looked at the strangers and decided, he should trust them. "I was taken from my village."

The woman gasped and turned towards the man. She whispered something to him. Hadi watched but couldn't make out what they were saying. The woman took Hadi's hand and led him to the perfume kiosk.

"Which perfume would you like to get?" she asked.

Hadi pointed to a bottle with amber colored liquid. "That one."

The woman bought it and handed it to Hadi. "Let us take you where you need to go."

"I need to find a boat that is going to Karachi," said Hadi.

"I know where there are boats," said the man. "I sailed in one myself to get here."

With Hadi between them, the woman and the man took him to the harbor. They went down side alleys, crossed streets and even took a short cut through a fancy hotel. *I would have never found it,* he thought. Hadi held tightly to the woman's hand. He couldn't believe his luck. The man walked up and down the boardwalk talking to different fishermen and pointing to Hadi. Finally, he called for the woman. "Come on, I found someone!"

Hadi and the woman rushed over. There was a man with a rickety boat, much like the one Hadi had arrived on. "This man has promised me to take you to Karachi and then help you find a ride to your home. I have paid him well, so you should be all set."

Hadi's eyes bulged. He smelled the salt-water drift passed his nose and grinned at the two strangers.

"Are you angels?" he asked.

The man and woman laughed. "I've never been called an angel before, or a movie star," said the woman. She knelt back down and made sure Hadi's goods were tucked in his shirt safely. Then she pulled out a small wallet and stuffed some money in Hadi's hand. "For your family." The woman looked as if she knew all the heartache Hadi had felt. Her blue eyes swelled with tears. "I'll pray that you have an angel with you making sure you safely return home."

Hadi stared into her blue eyes. They were like sapphires. "Thank you," he whispered.

"Come on, boy. We have a long trip ahead of us." The fisherman shook the fair skinned man's hand. Hadi hugged the woman around her waist and looked up at her.

"I will never forget you," he said. "Thank you." He saw a tear fall from her eye. She nodded and smiled.

Hadi shook the man's hand. "Thank you," he said. The fisherman had already boarded and Hadi quickly followed. The ropes were untied and the engines started with a loud grumbling noise. The sun was on its way down, leaving orange and pink streaks in the sky. Hadi leaned on a rail and waved at the couple standing on the dock. They waved back. The boat slowly backed away sending fumes of gas into the air.

"Bye!" shouted the woman.

Hadi waved. He waved until the strangers were little specks on the dock and his arm felt like it was about to fall off. The harbor, the city with its twinkling lights all grew faint. Hadi wondered what the couple was doing and whom they would help next. He was glad he put his trust in not just one person that day, but three. It felt much better than lying. The black night sky quickly overtook the pink and yellow sunset. Hadi gazed at the stars as they blinked one by one in the sky like he had done so many times before. The fisherman said nothing to Hadi. He focused on steering the boat.

Hadi had to believe that this man would take him where he needed to go. He had to trust the fisherman now too and that he would take care of him. He rested his head on his knees and slowly was lulled to sleep by the chug chugging of the diesel engine and the boat that would soon carry him home.

Chapter 13

Home At Last!

Hadi was awakened by a quick shake on the shoulder. He rubbed his eyes and looked about. A small oil lamp burned inside the cabin on the boat. The sky was still dark. He heard voices getting louder as the boat pulled into the dock. Hadi stood up and saw lights in the buildings along the shore. He turned to the fisherman, "Karachi?" he asked.

The fisherman nodded. Hadi looked again. He couldn't believe it. He was nearly home. His heart raced inside his chest. The boat rumbled to a stop and gently hit the side of the dock. The fisherman turned off the oil lamp and joined Hadi on the bow of the boat. He threw ropes over and the men standing on the dock tied up the boat. "Let's go," he said.

Hadi followed him down the gangplank to the dock. Some of the men greeted the fisherman, shaking hands and asking about the trip. Hadi stood back and listened. He wanted to get home so badly and wished the men would hurry up with their greetings. Finally, he heard the fisherman ask if anyone was going to Multan.

"I am," said a man in the back of the crowd.

"Could you take this young boy with you and make sure he gets to the city?" asked the fisherman.

A short stubby man in the back eased his way forward and looked at Hadi.

"Who is he?" asked the man.

The fisherman shrugged. "A boy some foreigners found in Abu Dhabi. They told me he was illegally brought over. Now I'm bringing him home. They asked if I could get him to Karachi, then help him find a ride home."

"I suppose, as long as he keeps quiet. What's your name, boy?" said the man. He had a cigarette hanging out of the corner of his mouth and it wiggled up and down as he spoke.

"Hadi." He looked back down at his feet, which he could barely see in the dark shadows below.

"Hadi. That's a nice name. It means *gift*. It's a long ride, maybe nine hours," said the man.

"I don't care," said Hadi. "I want to get home."

"Follow me." Hadi followed the man through the group of people over to a car parked on the side of the road. "Get in the back. I'll be your taxi ride." The man opened the door and smiled as Hadi got in.

Hadi scrambled to the far side of the car. He leaned his head against the seat and looked up at a ripped ceiling. Pieces of fabric hung down, some in his face. It was similar to the car that took him away so many months ago. He closed his eyes and listened to the car start. He felt the vibrations of the engine under him. His tummy growled a little, but Hadi has forgotten his hunger. He wanted to get home.

The car pulled out of the street and onto a main road. Hadi knew if he fell asleep the time would go faster. If he slept, though, the man might not take him home. *Can I trust him too?* thought Hadi. He looked at the man's reflection in the rearview mirror. His face was gentle and he hummed while he drove away from the city. It was late at night and both the driver and Hadi were tired. No one said a word the entire time. It was a long drive and the motion of the car rocked Hadi's head, making his eyes heavy and longing for sleep. He dozed for minutes at a time but also carefully watched where the man was taking him. *Soon*, he thought. *I should recognize something!*

Hadi sat up and looked out the window. Night turned into day. The streetlights slowly dimmed one by one. He watched people coming out of their homes to go to work. He watched the quiet road turn into a busy highway. He watched the palms sway in the breeze and the river flow beside the road. His country was awakening and everything seemed familiar and safe to Hadi.

Hours went by and the man stopped only once to get gas. Back in the car, they continued their journey. The villages became smaller and the arid land became more like a prairie. A few trees stood along the river and Hadi thought he saw mountains up ahead. *Could it be? Could we be close?* Hadi smiled as he stared out the window. Then he saw it. There to his left was the village where we had been kidnapped months before.

"Wait!" hollered Hadi. "Stop here! Please."

The man slammed on his breaks, causing the car to fishtail. A plume of dust rose up from behind the car.

"What's the matter with you?" shouted the man from the front.

"That village," said Hadi pointing. "I'm home!"

The man looked and shook his head. "That's no home to me,"

Hadi jumped out of the car and looked all about. "I'm home! I'm home!" he shouted.

There on his right was a small road, the dirt road that he walked on months before. Hadi knew just beyond was his home and his family, waiting.

"Thank you!" said Hadi, and he bolted down the dirt road.

"Your welcome!" said the man and he sped off. Hadi breathed deeply as he skipped along. He took off his sandals and felt the dirt road beneath his feet. The air was thick and wet and Hadi swore he would never complain about the sticky air again.

He heard the birds in the trees and watched a snake slither by in front of him. The air smelled sweet. He rounded the corner where he had kicked the dirt. Hadi laughed. He had forgotten about his fight with his mother. He remembered how angry he was at her for making him do simple chores. "How stupid I was," he said. "I'll never complain again. Nothing is as bad as being taken from your family and forced to work!" He ran the remainder of the road until his home came into view. No one was outside at first. Hadi looked anxiously for any familiar face. Then, from behind the house walked a woman carrying a bucket. A man and several children followed her. Hadi's heart leapt into his throat. He could hardly breathe as he jumped up and down waving his arms wildly.

"Mama! Papa!" he shouted and hurried towards them like he was a camel in a race. They looked up. Their eyes bulged wide.

His mother dropped the bucket and a wave of water poured out. She held open her arms and cried, "Hadi, Hadi, Hadi."

Everyone circled around him, giving kisses and hugs. Hadi never felt so great in all his life. Not even the cheers from the grandstands made him feel as important as his mother calling his name. He never wanted to be separated again. He sat outside his home with his family and told them all that he had been through. He had never seen his father cry. This day was different. Hadi's mother wouldn't let go of his hand. She gently stroked the side of his face. Hadi turned to her. "Mama. I'm sorry that I complained about everything. I'm sorry we fought."

Tears rolled down her wrinkled face like little streams tumbling down a mountainside. Her brown eyes, so tired looked lovingly at Hadi. "That doesn't matter now, Hadi. I thought I would never see you again. You're home finally, safe with us."

Hadi smiled and looked around. He took in the lush green trees, the smiling faces of his brothers and sister. He laughed when Samra squealed in delight. Hadi was finally home where he belonged. He looked forward to sleeping on the cold, hard ground that night nestled in between his family. He looked forward to his chores the next day. He even couldn't wait to jump in the river and let the water run over his body.

"If only Asim were here," he said. But he knew Asim was in a better place and probably looking down on Hadi with a big smile. Hadi was home and that was all that mattered.

The End

Some things to know:

Abu Dhabi—In 1971, six states—Abu Zaby, 'Ajman, Al Fujayrah, Ash Shariqah, Dubayy, and Umm al Qaywayn, merged to form the United Arab Emirates (UAE). Abu Dhabi is the capital city of the United Arab Emirates.

Arabian Sea—Also known as the Persian Gulf. Large body of water that separates several countries in the Middle East. Check this site for more information on the beautiful Arabian Sea:
http://www.arabiansea.com/

Dirham—the basic unit of money for the United Arab Emirates.

Hadi—his name means gift or guide.

Karachi—Is a large port in Pakistan on the Arabian Sea.

Matzoh—A type of unleavened bread.

Multan—Also known as the City of Saints. It is located in eastern central Pakistan, in the Punjab, near the Chenab River. Hadi comes from a village nearby Multan. He lives in an agricultural area of Pakistan.

Salwar—Pants that young boys wear. They taper at the ankles. A **kameez** are long shirts that go to their knees.

Souk—A market place. In this story, it is a camel market place where camels are bought and sold and taken care of by young foreign boys.

Some websites and addresses of organizations devoted to helping children:
(Note that because websites come and go quickly, these may not be accurate or online.)

1. **http://www.happychild.org.uk/dir/index.htm—Project Happy Child, devoted to exploited children around the world.**

2. **http://www.antislavery.org/archive/submission/submission 2002-UAE.htm**—article on trafficking camel jockeys to the United Arab Emirates.

3. **http://www.stophumantraffic.org/countrybg.html—article** on trafficking children for camel racing. Read about Irshad's story!

4. **http://www.savethechildren.org—**Save the Children charity website.
    Save the Children
    54 Wilton Road
    Westport, Connecticut 06880

5. **http://www.unicef.org—**The United Nations Children's Fund homepage.

    The United States Mailing Address:
    UNICEF House
    3 United Nations Plaza
    New York, New York 10017

The United Kingdom mailing address:
Africa House
64-78 Kingsway
WC2B 6NB London
United Kingdom

6. **www.camelraces.com**—a website devoted to educating peo-
    ple on camel racing.

7. **http://www.iabolish.com**—antislavery website
    Mailing Address:
    iAbolish
    198 Tremont St., #421
    Boston, MA 02116

Camel Facts:

Do camels store water in their humps? No, the humps on camels are really a giant mound of fat. They are the only animals that have humps. These humps of fat allow the camel to go for long periods without food or water. Sometimes up to two weeks!

Life span—camels live on average for 35 years but some have lived as long as fifty years.

Three eyelids? Yes, camels have three eyelids. In the desert, sand blows around a lot. Camels need these extra layers to help keep the sand out. They can also close their nostrils for the same reason. Too bad the riders of camels can't do the same!

Camels come in different shapes-some have one hump (Arabian) while others (Bactrian) have two! Hadi rode Arabian camels.

How tall, how wide? Camels can weigh between 700 and 1200 pounds and be seven feet high! They are huge compared to a small nine year boy weighing only 60 or 70 pounds.

Calf or Colt? A baby camel is called both!

Camels on US Stamps—camels have appeared twice on the United States stamps. The first was issued for the Fort Bliss Centennial Stamp. The camel is tiny on the stamp and you probably need a magnifying glass to find it. The second stamp was issued in 1988. It is a carousel camel.

The word camel—The word camel appears in the King James version of the Bible 45 times.

Another name? Camels are also called ships of the desert. Can you guess why? They can carry up to 400 pounds and travel 25 miles in one day.

Author's Notes

When I visited Abu Dhabi a few years ago, one of the places I visited was a camel souk or marketplace. I was immediately overcome with the heat, as it was 120 degrees Fahrenheit in the shade. Yet there is a beauty about the desert, the small villages and the lush green cities that make up the Arab landscape.

The souk was located about a half an hour beyond the beautiful city of Abu Dhabi, which is the capital of the UAE, United Arab Emirates. Unlike the beautiful city, the camel souk was dry, dusty and very brown. Only a few trees dotted the landscape. Before we even got there, desert stretched out all around us. Big wire fences lined either side of the road so that the wild camels wouldn't wander onto the road and be hit by passing cars and trucks.

I noticed that many young boys worked at the camel souk, but at the time didn't inquire why or who they were. I assumed, in my own ignorance, that they were young Arab boys. Only later did I find out that an Arab boy would never be allowed to race camels, let alone clean their corrals. These children were sent, kidnapped or brought to the Middle East to work. Sometimes they are as young as two years old. They grow up living in six foot square huts. They have no nationality and will never even know what language their parents spoke.

In response to international pressure, the UAE introduced a ruling in 1993 that children weighing less than 45kg could not be camel jockeys. However, if the camels belong to a Sheikh, rules don't apply.

"The United Arab Emirates are not alone in the practice of exploiting children in the name of sport. This practice is accepted in many Middle Eastern countries. When the children are no longer of any use to the sport, they may be sent to the country, which the authorities can only guess was their original home or they may join the ranks of "illegal" immigrants who form a cheap labor force." (www.camelraces.com)

I learned that many of the boys came from other countries like Pakistan, Bangladesh and parts of Africa in hopes of making more money for their families back home. Some, like Hadi, are even kidnapped from their homeland and sold to the owners of the camel souks to work. There is much concern about this and several human rights groups are trying to stop the illegal buying and selling of children, which doesn't just happen in Arab countries but all over the world.

Perhaps to many young boys, the thought of becoming a champion camel jockey is more appealing than begging on the streets. The harsh reality of it is that very few make it to the winner's circle, most work hard, are paid little and have no family life to speak of.

Sometimes their fathers, who hook up with agents from the camel souks, accompany the boys. Pakistan has tightened the laws on sending children to work in the camel racing business, but other countries haven't followed their lead.

In the past, boys as young as four, five and six would race the camels. They would be tied onto the camels. Sadly, there were accidents and since the young boys were unable to free themselves from the camels, some were crushed and killed. Today there are strict laws about how young a camel jockey can be. The legal age for a camel jockey is ten. These young boys are so small, they hardly look old enough to ride a bike. And even today, some boys are still tied to camels. They are also supposed to wear helmets that resemble bike helmets to protect their heads. One enterprising trainer decided to use Velcro on the saddles and the boys' trousers enabling the boys to stick to the saddles without falling off. If they needed to, they could escape easily.

The desert used to be the racetrack long ago, when Bedouin tribes would race for fun. Today modern racetracks with grandstands holding thousands of spectators are built for camel racing. Camel racing was a traditional sport of Bedouin tribes. Thousands of camels would race across the desert. Today, camel races are held during the fall and winter months and more than two thousand camels participate. Camel racing is one of the most popular events held. You can imagine the glory of winning a race!

But what about the boys? Yes, often they make more money than they would at home, but these young boys are working when they should be gaining an education; when they should be playing and making friends. And what about the young boys who race, risking their lives every time they ride a camel? Racing camels sell for anywhere from $150,000 to $1 million. Who is making the money? The boys are only getting a very small portion of it. At the end of the day, these boys are the ones suffering. They are part of an ongoing battle over child labor and the law. A friend of mine who lives in Abu Dhabi gave me these statistics and thought provoking question:

"Like everywhere else there are horror stories, however I should say these are few and far between now. As a family, the life is better for these kids and their fathers. They are racing for about 5 years from the age of 7 to 12. Usually they then go back home. They do get a better life than the poverty they see at home. On average the salary of the jockey would be US $200 per month and that of his father US $700 per month plus a room for both father and son. This compares with US $10 per month they would earn at home. However, it is a hard and indifferent life. In my opinion, it does not justify the child labor aspect of it. A good racing camel costs about US $150,000 and some have been bought for US$ 1 million. So, where is the money going?" Not to the boys.

In every country, there are crimes committed against children. For most people in the Arab world, selling children is criminal and most do not believe this should occur. In order to stop the selling of human beings, children and adults should be educated, which is why Hadi's story is being told.

0-595-29375-1

Printed in the United States
66069LVS00003B/183